New Wife's

Nude Beach Surprise

The Story of Sweet Catherine Book 3

Matt Coolomon

New Wife's Nude Beach Surprise

The Story of Sweet Catherine Book 3

Copyright © 2013 Matt Coolomon

Independently Published

ISBN: 9781519031501

The Girl Next Door

Jared

I shouldn't have been looking, the girl was virtually my sister – and not just my sister, but my little sister. And not by blood of course, but I'd watched her grow up next door and she has always treated me like the big brother she never had.

I glanced from her legs to her step-father looking at me. My face heated guiltily. We both glanced at young Catherine's exposed panties then connected eyes again. Bruce drew a breath and expelled, his head shaking, his eyes rolling disapprovingly as he strode past where I was sitting. "Come on!" he grumped at me.

I left the television and Catherine chatting and giggling with a girlfriend on her phone. She was on the other end of the lounge, with her legs bent up toward where I'd been sitting, her skirt tiny and her legs swaying open and closed as she fidgeted unknowingly.

3

"Sorry, Bruce, it's hard not to look sometimes," I explained as I caught up with my neighbour.

"Ha! Tell me about it! Wish the girl would put some damned clothes on."

"Yeah, I noticed Milton and Heath checking her out earlier too. I don't know if she plays up to it or not. I don't know how much is deliberate tease!"

Bruce set up a step ladder to the rafters of his garage, where he had a canoe stored. He had a buyer for it and had asked me to come over and help him get it down.

"Yeah, it's definitely tease, but worse lately since she dumped her last boyfriend, whatever his name was. She was down for about five minutes then bounced back full of beans and with her skirts and tops suddenly barely there!"

We lowered the canoe and carried it on our shoulders, up the driveway and to the front of the house.

"Oh my god, Daddy, what are you doing? Are we going canoeing?" Catherine sung from the lounge room window. She came out onto the veranda.

"No we're not going canoeing, love. I've got a buyer coming to pick this up today."

"Oh but why! I love canoeing. It's been ages since you took me!"

"Exactly, love, it's been years. And you never said anything. I thought you'd lost interest being all grown up now and too busy for your old man."

The girl glared. "Huh! You're the one who's always too busy, Dad." She turned on me with her cheeky little smile/smirk. "And when's the last time you offered to take me anywhere, Jared? Some make-believe big brother you are!"

I scoffed. "Yeah, like your dad said – you're too busy for either of us since you've been entertaining boyfriends this past few years."

"Boyfriends? Yeah right – you mean entertaining dickheads!"

Bruce and I laughed, Catherine had a giggle too. She came down the stairs and I had to look away from her nipples poking at her skimpy little boob-tube or whatever it was. They were pretty obvious through it and even visible in the sunlight.

"So, you're really selling it?" she mused, rocking the canoe on the grass with her foot. "I actually miss doing stuff like this with you guys, you know. If either of you ever asked me, I'd still want to."

Bruce shrugged. "Well, it's a bit late now, love, I've already sold it. Unless we just hire one for a weekend, I suppose?"

"Actually, I know of a free ticket to a white water rafting weekend, come to think of it," I suggested. "You remember my friend Foley?"

"Um, yes, I remember Foley," Catherine answered, blushing a little and chewing her smile.

"You remember Foley, don't you, Bruce? From over on 2nd Avenue. He used to hang around up until a few years ago when he moved away. Blond fellow."

Bruce shrugged, frowning. "Yeah I remember him. What about him?"

"No nothing, it's just that I was chatting with him last night and he was saying he broke up with his girlfriend

6

and they were planning a white water rafting thing this weekend – that he had a spare ticket that he couldn't get a refund on. He was asking if I wanted to go, but I can't, I'm working."

I looked to Catherine, still blushing excitedly and wringing her hands in front.

"Would you be interested, Cath?" I shrugged. "Could be fun!"

"Um yes, I'd be interested. Where is it?"

"It's up past Razorback. It's about three or four nights, rafting and camping. It's with a whole tour group, so good chance to make some new friends."

"And this Foley – what's he doing with himself these days?" Bruce asked pointedly.

"Dad!" Catherine scolded. "I'm sure he's fine if he's a friend of Jared's. You don't have to worry!"

Bruce rolled eyes at his step-daughter. "I'd worry less if you'd put some damned clothes on, you bloody little scamp!"

"Huh! What!" Catherine cried and looked down at herself, plucking at her top. "You old fuddy duddy, there's nothing wrong with my clothes. Not in this century!"

I laughed and left father and daughter to discuss that one. "I'll give Foley a call," I called back to Catherine. "I think he'd be picking you up tomorrow afternoon, is that okay?"

"Yes fine! Tell him I'd love to come, and I'll do the cooking if there's any."

Foley

"Shit!"

I let my apartment door click shut behind me and walked into the living room – stuff strewn everywhere – a set of keys, a red marking pen and a framed photo of me and Sandra on the coffee table in the middle of the room – Sandra scribbled out with the red marking pen.

I knew she was going to be picking up her stuff today but wasn't expecting this.

I picked up the photo and slumped on the lounge, pulled a book from beneath my arse and pushed it aside with a stack of CD's on the next cushion slewing onto the floor.

I took a big breath and expelled. There was a knot in my chest that rose to my throat and made me swallow hard at it and fight the urge to tear up. I had found out about Sandra cheating on me and told her to pack her shit and get out. I don't know, I'd kind of suspected something for a while now, but it still came as a shock when a mate called me the other night and told me to get down to the pub and see for myself.

I'd caught her on her way out of the pub, all over this other dude. She'd laughed in my face and went with him.

I was in love with the fucking bitch and she ripped my heart out.

There was a bottle of Bourbon on the floor. I twisted the top off and took a long pull on it, grimacing at the bite as I swallowed, but it was better than the feel of that knot in my throat.

I put the picture aside and rested back, tipping up the bottle and taking another big gulp. My phone buzzed in my pocket, jingling with a call.

"Hey, man." It was my buddy Jared.

"Hey, Foley, how you going?"

"Up the shit. Sandra trashed the place, man." I gulped. "She's gone though, eh. Good fucking riddance."

"Yeah sorry, man. You okay?"

I took a breath and huffed. "Yeah I'm okay. What's up anyway, wanna go to the pub?"

"No, aren't you going on that rafting thing tomorrow?"

"Oh that. Yeah, I dunno. Feel like a fucking loser turning up alone, eh!"

"Yeah sure, that's why I'm ringing, man. I've got a plus one for you, and she'll definitely brighten you up."

"She?"

"Yep, you remember young Catherine from next door?"

"Er.. Catherine... the blond chick?"

"Yup, she's just broken up with a boyfriend, so you've got that in common. I bumped into her today and thought of your spare ticket to ride. She'd be great company, man. Put a smile on anyone's face, she would!"

"Yeah but she's only a kid. How old is she?"

"Na, man, she just turned 20. She's no kid anymore." My friend chuckled. "Actually you ought to arrange it so Sandra sees you taking her along, buddy. That'll stick it to her, if you know what I mean!"

I'd only ever met Jared's neighbour chick once or twice a few years ago. She was a little hottie as a teen.

11

I scratched my head. "Yeah, man, but she's still pretty fucking young eh. I mean, are you um... are you saying I should um..?"

"No! Hell no!" Jared chuckled. "Mate, I'm saying you absolutely shouldn't..! This isn't a hook-up. The girl's like a sister to me. Her old man would kill me if I set her up with you as a fucking date or whatever. No, man, I mean just to hang out with and have a fun rafting ride. Just as friends!"

"Oh right." I gulped. "That's good then, I'm too fucking raw for anything else right now anyway."

"Well great. Perfect. The girl's gonna be good medicine. Trust me."

"Ha, yeah I guess. Plus I could at least send Sandra some photos, right?"

"Haha, that's what I'm saying, buddy. Doesn't matter that she's just a friend along for the ride. She's friendly as, and she'll look great beside you in some happy holiday snaps."

"Shit yeah. Hey this is good, man. Thanks for this."

"Na, it's cool. Just promise you'll look after her for me, okay? Her old man would seriously kill me if anything happened to her."

I thought a bit harder, just kind of remembering.

"He's a cop, isn't he – her old man?"

"Um yeah, but I'm just fucking with you, man. He's cool. He's a good guy."

"So, a copper's daughter then. Haha, this'll be fun." I had another swig of Bourbon. "So, I'll swing by and pick her up on my way then. Do you want to text me her number."

"Alright, man, you sure you're alright though? Want me to come around, or we could have a beer or two. You're not leaving until tomorrow arvo, yeah?"

"Yeah, no that's okay, man. I better tidy up here and see what's what. I'll be cool."

"Okay good, I'll go let Cath know and send you her number. Take it easy, man, and have a good trip eh!"

"Alright, cheers Jared. Thanks again for this, man. And see if you can get the girl on side with the photo's for me, okay! Haha that'll be fucking priceless."

Catherine

"Oh my god, how do you pack for a camping and rafting weekend with a hot guy you don't even know?"

I huffed and shook my head at everything I owned strewn all over my bed. The guy was too old for me anyway. I mean, as far as *that* went. He was too old to have an actual relationship with, but he just broke up and was probably going to be needing some female attention. He was probably going to want sex, which would be fine. I was perfectly willing to let him have me, since he was paying and all. It was going to be so fun riding rapids and camping out. I was definitely going to let the guy have sex with me if he wanted to.

I sorted some pretty pajamas. I decided it wasn't the place to be wearing satin or anything, and definitely not a negligee or teddy. They were more for hotel rooms or at a man's apartment. Pajamas were better suited to camping in a tent, but I had some pretty ones of those and sorted one satin pair, just in case things got romantic at all. Otherwise I decided on my two favourite bikinis, board

14

shorts and some tops and skirts for at night around the camp fire or whatever, also my hiking boots because Foley had said to bring some.

I wondered if Foley still had his hair the same, sort of scruffy and sexy looking. I loved his blue eyes and how muscly he was, even though he wasn't a big guy at all. I remember fantasizing about him a lot when he was around for a while a few years ago.

There was a knock on my door and Mum poked her head in. "I'm going to the shop, sweetheart, do you need anything for your holiday?"

"Um, I don't think so, Mum. I just need towels."

"Yes, I've put some out for you. And have you got plenty of sunscreen?"

I showed my mother through what I'd packed and she decided she'd pick up some travel size toothpaste and shampoo and conditioner for me. I ended up going to the shop with her, and by the time we got back, Foley was there at Jared's house next door. He was early though, so I took my time and had my last real shower for a few days, making sure I was shaved fresh everywhere and shaping my landing strip a bit narrower.

I wanted to look sexy in case Foley wanted me. The sound of him and Jared talking over the fence outside my bathroom window was thrilling me and making me take even longer getting ready.

He had a 4WD and I'd soon be sitting in the passenger seat beside him. I'd done this with guys before, and decided to wear a particular shirt that was button-up and the fabric gaped between the buttons when I sat down. There was a good view of my boobs in through the front of it when sitting in a car – a good view for the driver that was.

I put it on with no bra and left a button open at the top as well, to make sure he'd get a good look. I had on cut-off jean shorts and my sandals and sunglasses. The men were milling around the 4WD as I approached, and Daddy took my backpack and put it in the car.

"Hey," Foley said, smiling huge. His hair was just like before and he was unshaven and *ohmygod his eyes!*

"Hi," I said back and felt my face and neck flush.

"Okay take care, love." Daddy said and hugged me then opened the passenger door for me to climb up into the car. "Look after my girl!" he called over to Foley, making me flush with real embarrassment now.

I glared and scolded. "Dad!"

"You bet, sir, I'll take care of her," Foley called back and gave me a wink.

Ohmygod he's so hot!

"Okay have fun!" Jared called to me from looking in the driver's side window, his gaze flashing up from where my shirt was already gaping and showing my boob and hard nipple.

Foley had a look too but quickly put on his sunglasses. Then as we drove and chatted, I noticed his eyes sometimes rolling down and to the side to look at me some more, and I made sure I kept my shirt bunched and gaping so there was a good view for him.

"So, you just broke up too, Jared was saying?"

"Oh yeah, but that was nothing," I answered quickly. "It was just some boy from work. It didn't really mean anything."

17

"Oh right. Yeah it turns out mine didn't mean anything either, I suppose. Not in the end."

"Oh? What happened? Why did you break up?"

The guy shrugged. "We were probably never right for each other. I guess she just realized it before I did."

"Hmm, did she cheat on you?" I probed. Jared had sort of hinted when I was grilling him.

Foley shrugged again – nodded a little – kept his eyes straight ahead.

"Sorry," I offered softly. "Are you sad?"

"Huh, I guess. I'll snap out of it though. We're gonna have fun yeah!"

"Um yes! This is gonna be great. I'm so grateful you invited me, Foley."

He glanced and I just kept staring and chewing my lip. His eyes flashed down to my open shirt and back up. He blushed.

I looked down and fiddled with the undone button. "Sorry, it's this silly shirt."

"No, it's pretty. Suits you."

I smiled – stared back as he glanced again. I released the button I was fiddling with but left it undone. His amazing blue eyes flashed down then back to the road again, then he did a double take. "Oh shit."

I bit on my smile. Guys are so easy and they're all the same. I'd recently been for a week-long holiday on this old island with a group of local boys all over me, as well as the old fishermen perving at me all the time. I was used to it and liked playing up to all these naughty men now.

"Sorry about my dad."

Foley grinned. "Oh right. Yeah, he's a bit scary."

"Hmm, but he's harmless." I grimaced a little. "Plus he actually approves now."

"Approves?"

"Uh huh, of me, and of guys."

I got looked at again. "Of guys?"

"Uh huh, of guys wanting to have sex with me, and of me letting them."

Foley gulped – his eyes flashing to my chest and back up again. "Of you letting them?"

"Hmm, I like letting guys. It's fun and feels nice, don't you think?"

"Er... yeah, I guess."

"Plus it's perfectly natural. We were made to fit together in such an exciting way, and especially with you men and how much you absolutely *need* it. You're all pretty hopeless like that. Or all the guys I meet seem to be."

"Yes but there's more to it than just the physical. There's a whole relationship side of it too."

"Ha!" I scoffed. "Tried that a bunch of times and so have you by the sound of it. I don't see why there has to be anything more than the physical."

The guy looked me up and down again.

"Well do you?" I challenged him.

"Holy shit." He gulped and looked at me again. "Seriously?"

"Um no, that's the whole point. I mean not-seriously. Just for fun, and if you need it from me at all." I was blushing and just clinging to my fading confidence now. "I mean, just so you know I'm willing, if you want."

"Aw fuck!" I got eyeballed again – up and down. "Don't worry about your dad, Jared would kill me first."

I giggled. "Jared's a pushover too. Let me worry about Jared."

"Ha! Sure! And you're seriously saying what I think you're saying? Right up front?"

"Hmm, well, up-front is the best way to be, isn't it?"

"And you're talking about..?" He deliberately looked down my body and back up again.

"Uh huh, you said you wanted pictures, right? How crappy would they be if it was only acting!"

"Oh shit!"

I giggled again – turned in my seat and rested back against the door with my legs bent up – showing them to him. "Unless you don't want to," I challenged him again.

Foley

I could see the girl's panties up the leg of her jean shorts. "There's not going to be any question about me wanting it," I told her. "Fuck, of course I'm going to want to, but I still don't get it. We don't even know each other and you're saying you'll have sex with me?"

"Well, we don't exactly know each other, but we're going to be camping together, aren't we! Maybe even sharing a tent?"

"Er yeah, the tour group provide tents. I'm not sure how they work out who's with who."

"Hmm, but as far as they know, we're a couple right? So I'm guessing we'll be sharing."

"Yeah probably." I wasn't going to argue. I definitely wanted to be sharing with this chick. I had another look over her. I couldn't see her tits from front-on but her shirt was still gaping at the top and promising another look as soon as I had a better angle again.

"I can't help it if I like men," she started sweetly. "I love how strong and demanding you can all be, and I love how desperate you get. It's so amazing to feel that and be desired and taken hold of."

I just swallowed hard and looked at the girl.

"My girlfriends think I'm a slut, but I just think it's so natural and the way it's supposed to be."

I gulped again. "Oh yeah?"

"Uh huh, it's not just with anyone walking along the street, but if the situation occurs that there's a man close to me for some reason, then I think it's only fair if he gets aroused and needs it from me." She rubbed down her inner thighs and squeezed her hands between her knees. "I really like teasing men with how I dress, but in doing that I feel obliged to let them enjoy between my legs or in my mouth – to get a release after I've teased them. I think men deserve that from me, and by accepting your invitation like this, I know I'm going to be close to you and you might need a release when we're alone in our tent or whatever.

"Aw fuck," I groaned. I was boning up now. The girl looked at me trying to conceal it with my arm. She was smiling.

"See!" she said sweetly. "You're already starting to need it, aren't you!"

I took a breath and expelled. "Yeah I guess."

"Hmm don't worry, it's okay. I love it even more when the guy gets all worked up and crazy for it all during the day and loses it when he finally gets a chance at night. I love how hard you cum after having to wait."

"Aw shit, I can't believe this. You're just fucking teasing, aren't you? You're not serious?"

The girl shrugged. "You'll have to wait and see, I suppose. How far is it? What do we have to do today exactly?"

"Um..." I huffed a big calming breath. "It's not far to drive. We meet up with the tour group at the base of Razorback, we'll be there in about fifteen minutes. Then there's a bus ride up into the mountains that takes about four hours, and apparently we make camp for the first night by the river. Then we've got another three days rafting back to where we started. And there's camp sites with amenities along the way."

"Oh good. Amenities. I like amenities!"

We shared a laugh and got to chatting about her work and mine for the last bit of our drive. The tour group was about 30 people, an even split of men and women between Catherine's age and a bit older than me. Most were in solid groups of 4, which filled a raft and tent. That was the split. There were a few all-girl groups though, and we ended up grouped with another 2 single men. Paul and Mario were their names, both about my age, early 30's, and they seemed pretty cool.

"Are you sure this is okay?" Paul checked with Catherine for the third time, after the tour organizers had already made sure she was comfortable sharing with men.

"I don't mind at all, you guys! It's better than sharing with bitchy women, and as long as I'm allowed privacy to get changed and you guys aren't too loud or smelly at night!"

We all laughed.

"Ha! Hope the tent's got good flaps eh!" Paul teased his buddy. "Have to put you near the door."

"Yeah don't worry about me. I've got spare ear plugs for his snoring!" Mario shot back.

"Oh good, I'll have some please!" Catherine joined in, siding with the huge hairy Greek man.

We stuck together as a group on the bus and got to know each other, making friends well enough that it was looking like it would be a fun few days on the river.

I don't know if I was relieved or not that we ended up without much privacy. I was still in shock over how open and sexual Catherine was. There was no doubt I'd want to fuck her, but there was also the pressure of having to perform when she seriously intimidated me.

Our first night camping went well. It was a huge tent with plenty of room to have your own corner. There were eyes all over Catherine during the campfire dinner and the couple of drinks we were allowed afterwards. Once she was in pajamas in our tent, the three of us men had trouble looking anywhere else, and she knew it and played up to it.

"Hmm, night, boys," she said sweetly and pulled up her bed clothes to her chin. "It's going to be so fun tomorrow. I can't wait!"

That first night was as we had been warned. Mario farted in his sleep and Paul snored. I exchanged looks with Catherine in the moonlight and she teased me with her feet touching mine. I'm pretty sure I was erect all night, and certainly woke up that way.

Waking up was at first light though, and we were soon packed and had our gear loaded in a truck, to meet us at the first campsite down river. We then had a good day paddling with a gentle current and only a few mild rapids, as our tour guide Roger explained.

"Yeah that was practice, folks. Tomorrow we earn our stripes and day three is the test."

I had an instant dislike for Roger. He struck me as an arrogant prick, and I didn't like the way he was looking at Catherine all the time – trying to get her away from us guys and coaching her how to paddle and shit – getting fucking handsy with her!

The second night in out tent, things got a bit interesting. I had dozed off early as I was pretty fucked from all the paddling and ended up halfway drunk from my allotted three beers. I sort of woke up through the night and could swear Paul was jacking off. There was the unmistakable thumping under his covers and a strained breath or two at the end of it.

Then half an hour later I heard the same coming from Mario's corner of the tent, and I lay there stock still and listened to be sure, with Catherine's feet bracing against mine and the feel of her body shuddering or something until I heard a definite squelch of her wetness and her slender form tensed and softly quaked in the moonless darkness.

Foley

The ride down the rapids that next morning had been exciting but short. We had made camp for lunch and were on a hike with some of the men in our group. The tour guide Roger had eyes all over Catherine again.

"I think it's about time to head back," I said, helping her up and leading her away down a trail.

We walked in silence for a while with the other guys drifting back a bit.

Finally Catherine spoke. "I thought you liked the idea of seeing me with another guy."

"That was just talk when we were half drunk last night. And anyway, I thought you didn't like the idea here like this with more than just me."

Catherine smiled. "Well, it's different in real life."

"Got that right!" I admitted.

"So, you want me to stop, then?" Catherine asked softly.

I looked back at the others. "No, I don't want you to stop completely."

Apart from wanting to fuck the girl myself, I'd been fantasizing about Paul getting onto her as well. He was definitely picking up on her sense of sexual freedom.

"Then what?" she asked flatly. "Should I stop flirting? Are you getting jealous?"

"Aw fuck, I dunno – it's just that they were about to jump you back there!"

"And you don't like that guy Roger?"

"Not much!" I confessed. "He's a bit of an arsehole."

"What about Paul?" Catherine pressed, squeezing my arm.

"Yeah, he's okay and so is Mario."

"Well, I don't know if I want things to go any further either, but what about last night? Did you notice anything?"

"The way you rubbed one out in the dark?" I ventured, chuckling.

"Yes! Exactly that! I mean, I couldn't help myself after listening to them do it."

"What – listening to the guys jerk off?"

Catherine lifted to kiss my cheek lightly as we walked. "Yes that! And also because I was wet all day."

"Coz you were wet?" I queried stupidly.

The girl giggled. "No, not wet. I mean *wet*! Just teasing them and the way some of the guys were looking at me was making my legs wobbly all day, and then in the tent with you three guys and just me!"

"And today?" I asked after a moment's thought. "What would you have done if they did try to fuck you back there on the grass?"

We had stopped for a rest on top of the trail and the guys had been playing around with Catherine a bit, trying to get onto her.

"You mean all three of them?" Catherine uttered softly, her little fingers again squeezing where she was holding onto my arm.

It had just been Paul and Mario, and our guide Roger. It was the first time we had Catherine away from the rest of the group though. The tease had escalated quickly.

"Yeah, all three! Would you have let them?" I pressed anxiously, but managed a casual tone.

31

Catherine took a moment to answer. "The truth?" she finally said, peering up at me.

"Yeah! Be honest."

"Well, to tell the truth, when you said it was time to go back, I was just wondering about condoms – if they would've brought any with them, or whether to just let them anyway and risk them getting me pregnant."

"So, you would've let them?" I concluded. I could feel my face and neck flushing. My cock was flexing too though – just at the thought.

"Well, I don't know for sure. I was thinking about it, but only because of the way they were all staring at my legs. But if any of them actually tried anything, I don't know if I would have chickened out or not."

"Hmm – and how could they avoid staring? You were giving them a good enough look," I teased and dug my fingers into the girl's sides.

Catherine squealed and ducked away grinning back, and I ended up walking the last bit of the trail alone with my thoughts and the odd but nice feeling that I had been kind of adopted as a temporary boyfriend by a very attractive blond.

I honestly didn't know what I would have done if the other guys had tried to fuck her. I had fantasized about her a lot, but the reality was a very different and far more intense proposition. I ended my thoughts on the matter hoping I hadn't discouraged her from still showing off a bit at least.

*

Lunch was just a small snack because our guide had warned the afternoon would be a bit rough on the river. He also banned any alcohol for the few hours before setting off. Me, Catherine and our raft buddies Paul and Mario worked together to pack camp and load up. We paddled out into the river about mid-afternoon for what was to be a three-hour trip over mostly white water. Catherine had dressed in her bikini and board shorts with a short red tank top. She did look a bit more conservative, I thought, but soon enough the state of the river ended any deliberations about that.

We rode the frothy turbulent water for at least two hours, paddling for our lives and at times simply clinging to the side of the raft and praying. The rapids eventually ended though, and while we were drifting along recovering, our guide paddled past and told us there was just another hour of calm water to that night's camp.

We all stripped off the life gear and the conversation centered on the ride. Neither Paul nor Mario had been rafting before either, so we were all babbling about it like a bunch of kids, but soon enough the mellow water calmed things down and the last of the tour party paddled past.

"I suppose we should start paddling ourselves," Mario suggested, and he nudged Paul to pick up his oar.

"Do you guy's mind if I just relax and let you paddle?" Catherine asked.

Paul chuckled. "Guess not. But I didn't see you doin' much paddling before either. Weren't you the one clinging to the side of the boat with your eyes shut for the last couple of hours?"

"Yes," Catherine admitted frankly. "But it was scary, and anyway I just want to do some sunbathing for a little while now. Do you mind?"

"Hell no! We don't mind," Paul answered immediately, his eyes dropping to Catherine's chest and holding there while she gathered the hem of her top.

Mario was watching too as they both paddled slowly. They'd set the oars through the side supports and worked them while facing back. Catherine wrung out her top and laid it over the side of the raft, then without looking up, she pulled the string behind her back and lifted her bikini top over her head. She wrung it out too and laid it out to dry, her bare breasts wobbling freely beneath her arms. And like the other two men, I just watched in silence.

Her skin was lightly tanned but her breasts were pure white. Her nipples were erect too, of course, having just been freed from wet clothing. She looked down at them and carefully picked a piece of grass from her soft skin, catching it with a fingernail and brushing it from above her left nipple.

"Careful you don't burn," Paul said, and Catherine looked up at him.

"Thanks." She smiled a little. "I like your tan. It suits you."

"Mine? Yeah, I get around without my shirt on quite a bit, so it's more by accident than design. But it's good to see *you're* not too brown. Doesn't suit women."

Catherine smiled teasingly. "Oh, really? Maybe I should cover up?"

"Well, I wouldn't say that." Paul chuckled, but he was blushing a little and staring directly at Catherine's breasts.

"Can you slow down a bit then so we don't get too close to that next boat?"

"Sure! Happy to!" Paul answered and met Catherine's smile fully.

"And don't go blabbing to all the guys either!" Catherine went on, looking from Paul to Mario as she started undoing her board shorts. She undid the studs and gathered the waistband then paused to look up at them again. "Promise?" she teased sweetly.

I could see the lacy white fabric through her open shorts. The other two men offered something of a nod, and Catherine arched and rolled her shorts down. She pulled them past her knees and slipped them from her ankles.

"Are they swimmers?" Mario asked her, and she smiled and blushed a little.

"No. It's uncomfortable wearing a bikini under these shorts," she explained, and she rested back and pulled her little wet panties up and smoothed them.

We could clearly see her pubic hair through the soaked lace, and between her legs the fabric was furrowed and clinging to the folds of her pussy. She laid back with one leg slightly bent and scissored across the other, but still the form of her opening was obvious. Catherine's pussy was smoothly shaven, with only a fine patch of hair above it, her slit quite pronounced with the wet fabric clinging as it was.

I lit up a smoke and pretended to watch the shoreline drifting past. Paul and Mario rowed along quietly looking at Catherine. She'd placed her top over her eyes and lay there in front of us for about 20 minutes, until we were approaching camp and Mario let her know.

Catherine sat up, but she didn't immediately get dressed. Instead, she brushed her hair while we all watched her breasts moving about. The guys had stopped paddling and were making no attempt at subtlety anymore.

Paul motioned to the far shore from camp and a little alcove where the water was quite still. "No rush, eh. Let's just paddle over there, man," he said to his buddy, and they resumed padding and guided us out of the current. "Yeah that's good, there's still a bit of sunlight yet and plenty of time to set up our tent." He looked at Catherine's tits. "You want to sunbathe for a bit longer?"

Catherine blushed up from her bare chest. "Um, okay, if you guys want me to."

"Oh yeah, we want you to alright," Paul said evenly and deliberately looked from her bare tits to her little panties.

"Hell yeah, we want you to," Mario added and gulped hard.

Catherine smiled and looked to me. She rested back and arched her chest. "I guess as long as I'm not teasing you men too much. I don't like to only tease."

I held her gaze and the challenge in it. I felt Paul staring and probably trying to figure out what was going on exactly.

I took a breath and expelled. "Yeah, she doesn't like to be a tease," I said. "She doesn't like getting guys all worked up and not seeing that through, do you?" I challenged back.

The girl's blush fired up and she peered from one of us to the other.

"So, are you guys actually together?" Paul asked.

"No, just friends," I answered.

I had decided I wanted this to happen. To hell with the consequences back home with Jared, I wanted to fuck this chick and wanted to watch these other dudes get onto her as well.

"So, just friends eh," Paul echoed, grinning as he touched Catherine's lower leg with his foot, pressing against it and getting her to part her bent up knees.

Mario tilted to have a look between her legs as well. I did too.

"But you *are* teasing us," Paul went on. "This is definitely a tease, eh buddy!"

Mario gulped again. "Yep, definitely."

My chest and entire body flushed with tingles. "Not if she lets us all have some of that," I said.

"Yeah true, not if she lets us all have some of it," Paul echoed again. "What do you say, baby?"

"Hmm, I'll let you all if you like," Catherine uttered. "But not here like this – not until we're in our tent tonight, okay?"

"Aw fuck yeah," Paul groaned.

"All of us?" his friend asked excitedly.

"Um yes, of course," Catherine went on sweetly. "It wouldn't be fair for any of you to miss out and have to do it for yourself anymore. I think it's only right that I let you have me and enjoy the feel inside of me when you cum. I think men should get to have that, and women should allow it if they agree to sleep in the same tent like we are." She peered around at each of us. "It's why I took my clothes off like this – to excite you all and make your big balls start filling – since you're all being so nice to me and deserve me to be nice back to you."

"Ooh yeah, you're gonna be so nice to us," Paul groaned and rubbed up her leg.

She squeezed her thighs together, giggling and scolding, "Um, but not here, I said!"

"Oh hell, let's go set up the tent then!" Mario groaned anxiously, and we all laughed.

*

Camp was at the base of a steep, densely timbered slope, and we pitched tents on the flattest section on the bank of the river. As had been the case the previous night, there were amenities buildings and the meal was good. After dinner Catherine spent an hour chatting with some of the women then slipped into the tent. It was still quite early, but I left the group of guys and followed her, and before I reached the tent, Mario and Paul caught up with me.

"Can we come in?" Paul asked before entering.

"Of course," Catherine said cheerily. She was folding her clothes from the day and packing them.

Mario and Paul made their beds, and I helped Catherine then grabbed a deck of cards I'd brought along. The guy's joined me in a few hands, but Catherine wanted to read, and she settled back against her pack with her knees bent up and her short dress falling nicely away from beneath. She'd changed for pink panties, and us guys had a game where we would try to push her foot aside a little further and she would pretend to resist.

After only a short time reading she folded her book and put it away. "Can you close the tent flap for me please, Mario? I want to get ready for bed."

"Should we go for a walk?" Paul asked her.

"No, it's your tent too, you guys can stay. But just let the flap down because those men out there can see right in."

Mario released the flap, and we all looked to Catherine. "Should we close our eyes or what?" Paul asked, grinning.

"No. You don't have to close your eyes." She smiled back at him, with her cheeks reddening as she bravely held his gaze. "I don't mind if you watch," she uttered, and she reached up beneath her dress and peeled her panties down her thighs. She was kneeling, and she lowered them until they were at her knees. Then she reached around back and unzipped her dress, catching it as it slipped from her shoulders and holding it over her breasts while she looked from Paul to Mario. "Promise you won't go blabbing to all the others?"

Paul swallowed hard. "We won't!"

Catherine released her dress and it fell to her knees. Her hands lowered to her sides and her fingers lightly touched her thighs. She watched the two men for a moment, their eyes wide and roaming her body slowly. She smiled lightly. "So, maybe you'll have something to think of when you're playing with yourselves next time?"

"Fucking oath!" Paul stated, and Catherine went bright red. "And how about you?" he added, grinning at her.

"I'm so wet right now," she breathed, and her eyes turned to me.

"Show us," Paul said evenly.

Catherine held my gaze, and I nodded. She looked back to Paul. "Do you guys have condoms?"

He shook his head, and we all looked to Mario, who shook his head as well. "We're both clean, though," Paul assured, turning to me then looking back at Catherine.

Catherine's eyes lowered for a moment before lifting again. "Okay then," she uttered.

"Are you sure?" I asked her. It was the end of any resistance I had left.

She was blushing sweetly. "Yeah, I think so."

"I'll pull out if you like," Paul offered, slipping a little closer. He touched Catherine's thigh, running his fingers between her legs and stroking slowly up and down.

Catherine shrugged. "But that's the best bit."

"What is?" Paul pressed, knowingly.

"You know – when a guy gets really hard and it starts to throb inside me."

"You like that, do you?" Paul groaned, and his fingertips slipped up into Catherine's opening, easily penetrating her. Her eyes closed, and she gripped his shoulders and parted her knees as far as her panties and dress would allow. Paul inserted his middle finger, holding it there as she writhed down against his palm. Her face strained, her hips bucked, and her breasts wobbled and bounced until she suddenly tensed and ground herself forcefully down onto Paul's hand.

"Uhh...huhh," she moaned, digging her nails into his shoulders, and her eyes opened wide as her head shot back.

"Fuck she's tight," Paul declared, looking to me then back at Mario.

Catherine still convulsed. Her entire body would spasm at any movement of Paul's hand, and when his lips closed over a nipple, her head rocked forward and her eyes settled upon mine. "Is this okay?" she whispered.

She looked to Mario, with her eyes half closing and her hand cupping the back of Paul's head as he suckled her right breast. She slipped her dress and panties to her ankles and withdrew one foot. Then she collapsed back on her bed and spread her legs wide, pulling Paul down on top. His erection was poking at the waistband of his boxers, and he managed to free it as he forced himself between Catherine's thighs. The head of Paul's penis was swollen and shiny. I squeezed my own erection as I watched it open Catherine's cunt and sink into her.

Paul pumped her hard and fast, her legs bouncing either side of his hips. He was propped over her, holding her wrists together above her head and watching her breasts jolt. The muscles in his back were taut and his thighs clenched each time he humped up into her. His action suddenly slowed, though, and he held still with the head of his penis just parting her labia. "Are you sure?" he breathed hoarsely. "I'm fucking close!"

"Yes, I'm sure," Catherine uttered softly. "You can cum in me," she said, smiling teasingly, and Paul slowly opened her again. He measured one full stroke then held firm and pumped her a few times rapidly.

"Aw fuck – here it is!" he cried, and his balls clenched. He arched up and watched his penis. "Can you feel that?" he gasped, humping forcefully one more time and holding again.

"Mmm," Catherine moaned, her wrists slipping from his hand and her fingers moving to his buttocks and softly squeezing. "Mmm, I can feel it so well," she said, peering up at us other men. "I love it when a man cums in me."

Mario and I were both leaning around, and with Paul arched back, we were all watching his penis flex. He withdrew again so that only the head was inside of her, and although his shaft had softened a little, the veins were still engorged and the dome was still swollen and a deep shade of pink as it slipped out of my buddy's pretend sister I was supposed to be taking care of.

Paul smiled. "One very big load successfully deposited!"

Catherine giggled at that. "Well, it felt like it was squirting straight into my belly, so I would say – very successfully deposited," she said, but her eyes closed as he entered her again. Her mouth opened slightly as her knees lifted, and her body arched up off the thin mattress. She braced like that, and Paul got to his knees, wrapping his hands under her thighs and spreading her legs wide, lifting her up to him.

Catherine's hands clutched his forearms while Mario and I watched his penis slide in and out of her. Paul was leaning and craning his neck too so he could see their coupling.

"Uhh..huhh," Catherine uttered suddenly. Her head arched back and her eyes shot open. Her hands gripped the sheet and twisted into it as her body convulsed again.

"Fuck you can really feel it when she cums, can't ya?" Paul said to me. He was pressed firmly forward, and when Catherine's convulsions ebbed he withdrew from her.

*

Catherine collapsed and rolled onto her side with her hand slipping between her legs as she pressed them together. She lay there with her eyes closed, and from behind we could see her finger tips over her vagina and a trickle of fluid seeping from her and dripping down onto the sheet.

Paul had collapsed as well. He was sprawled on the floor with his boxers pulled up unevenly. Mario was on his hands and knees, and Catherine's eyes opened as he lifted her leg. He rolled her onto her back, and she looked up at me as this other complete stranger edged between her thighs and stretched his briefs down over a short but very thick erection. Mario lay down on top of her, and her forehead furrowed as he entered her.

"Ouch! Not too rough," she cried under her breath, her hands going to his shoulders and pressing against them a little. "Just gently until I get used to how big you are."

Her legs were limp, and Mario lifted one and held it aside, with Catherine's gaze again meeting mine as the guy started to slowly hump her. Her expression was blank, and after a moment she turned away and watched the side of the tent – her chin bouncing on Mario's thick, hairy shoulder and her hands slipping down his arms to come to rest flat upon the sheet.

Mario's round body covered her completely, and his fat hairy buttocks shook with each thrust of his pelvis until finally he groaned and held firm. Catherine's head

49

turned, her eyes fixing on the peaked roof of the tent while the thick cock inside her pulsed and gushed semen. She looked to me and held my gaze, the penis in her still throbbing quite powerfully.

Mario's body eventually relaxed, and he rolled to the side and lay there with his arm over his face and his chest heaving. His other hand was covering his genitals. Catherine closed her left leg over her right. Her dress and panties were still around her right ankle, and with the two sated men staring up at the tent roof, she sat and untangled them, slipping her left foot through and kneeling and tugging them up. While she straightened them though, a wet spot appeared and quickly soaked the gusset.

She was examining it when Paul said, "Oops!" and she blushed and smiled. "Should have told you about him," he added with a chuckle.

"Shut up!" Mario complained, rising to an elbow and searching for his briefs.

"What?" Catherine asked curiously.

"Well, there was this girl we both dated, and she told me about him. She said he cums about a bucket full, but he's so short and thick that it just drips back out," Paul explained.

"Ah fuck, ya prick! Don't tell 'em that!" Mario flopped back down, covering his face with an arm again.

Catherine peeled aside the edge of the fabric to show it was pasted with thick creamy semen. She was on her knees studying the mess, and as we all watched, another thick glob oozed from her slit and dripped to the floor of the tent. "Mario!" she scolded, smiling down at him as she replaced the fabric and smoothed it up into her opening.

The guy peered sheepishly from beneath his arm. "Sorry!"

Catherine sat back and had another look down the front of her panties, while I angled for another look too. The pink fabric was absolutely saturated and peeled from her slit as she held the waistband open. "It's so thick!" she uttered, then she smoothed the band in place and again mashed the sodden fabric up into herself. "Do you mind if I don't clean up?" she asked, meeting my eyes.

"What, are you worried about the guys out there?" Paul asked. There was still a gathering that sounded quite drunk just outside the tent.

"No," Catherine answered, shrugging and looking away as she lay down.

"So you just like the feel of it?" Paul pressed, and Catherine pulled the sheet up over her head.

"Maybe," she said from beneath it.

"Fair enough," Paul concluded and patted me on the back before pulling his own sheet up.

Mario crawled away, and I turned off the lamp and slipped into Catherine's bed beside her. She rolled away from me but wriggled back, and as I spooned in behind, she searched for my erection and poked it through the edge of her panties, guiding it to her sopping cunt. "Do you mind me being wet from them like this?" she whispered.

I kissed her neck, screwing her nice and slow. "No, I don't mind." She was squirming back onto me, and I could feel her wetting my balls with the other guys' cum. "Although, I might need a shower afterwards," I added with a chuckle, and both other men chuckled too.

"Don't blame me," Paul said. "Mine's nice and deep in her."

Catherine joined them laughing, though she was still squirming back onto my dick. "Don't take any notice of them, Mario. I felt some of yours squirting deep in me too. They're just jealous because you had so much more for me."

"Damn straight!" Mario declared.

Paul chuckled teasingly. "I've got some more for you if you want, baby."

"Yeah, have to wait your turn, though," I said, grinding up behind Catherine and making her moan a little.

She arched right back to whisper into my ear. Her breath was ragged and hot. "What if I lick you clean afterwards? Would that do instead of a shower?"

"Aw fuck, balls too?" I groaned, crushing her and screwing deep.

"Uh huh," Catherine moaned softly. "I want to lick it all up."

"Aw fuck!" I groaned again, and that time I drove up into the girl and ejaculated. I crushed her to my body and throbbed inside of her, flooding her and slopping her up even more than she already was. She had relaxed onto me, and I kept hold of her with her upper leg pulled back while I finished off grinding my clenched up balls into her wetness.

Paul chuckled. "Another successful deposit?"

"Fuck yeah!" I shot back at him, and all three of us men carried on laughing and ribbing each other.

Catherine remained quiet, pressed back against me and flaring her hips to keep in position for my cock still gently pulsing inside of her.

"So, was it a successful deposit?" Paul asked her after a while.

"Yes," she answered. "Feels nice and warm in my belly."

"Do you want another one?"

"No," she said sweetly. "You have to save up until tomorrow night."

The three of us men laughed and cheered, and Catherine lay there quietly while we chatted, and after a little while she slipped under the sheet and we all shut up. We remained silent while she licked and softly sucked my dick and balls clean, moaning a little as I held the back of her head and thrust into her mouth.

"Enough of that!" she scolded when I started getting carried away though, and she pushed me out of her bed and pulled her sheet up to her neck. "You can have more tomorrow night too, okay. All three of you can have turns with me again for our last night tomorrow."

"Aw fuck yeah, balls are gonna be full again by then," Paul said and chuckled.

"Hmm, well, I won't mind how full they are and how much you all pump into me like this again. I just hope you don't get me pregnant, though I think I should be safe."

Catherine

I was used to keeping track of my cycle and working out when I was safe to have unprotected sex. I was pretty sure I'd be okay right then, and the slight risk just made it all the more exciting. Also the fact that this was with complete strangers added to the intensity for me.

I know I'm a slut. Well, by definition, I am!

The thing is though, I just think it's perfectly natural to let men have sex with me. It all started with boys at school and then with my first job at a supermarket and the boys there. Just the way they were all so excited to look at me or touch me. Then my first actual sexual intercourse was with a mature man, and since then there have been a few other older man as well.

I just can't resist grown men. I can't move when they look at me and my legs turn to jelly if they touch me.

Then there was this holiday recently where I let these island boys have me over and over again, and since then I can't resist men or boys!

So yes, I certainly fit the description of a slut, but it just wouldn't have been fair to Paul and Mario if I didn't let them have sex with me. I understood about the way men got hard and they developed a serious need to have a release. I understood too that they could do it for themselves, but it had to be so much nicer if a girl did it for them. And I loved the way they got so excited and demanding.

I've always thought that there's a reason we girls are sort of soft and delicate, and there's a reason we like to be and feel that way. Ever since I've been old enough, I've understood we are a perfect match for each other. And I just think it's wrong for men to have to touch their big hard dicks themselves.

That's definitely a girl's job!

I just love doing it for guys. I love dressing to show them how soft and delicate I am, and when they get excited by that, I feel it's my responsibility to let them rub their hard cocks against me, or stick them inside of me – where it's all soft and delicate and wet and warm for them.

I so loved the thought and feel of being full of sperm from three different men that night in the tent, but I was asleep in no time and woke early the next morning all sticky between the legs and with such a strong after-taste of their yucky man cum in my mouth.

It had been fun riding the rapids the past few days but I was kind of over it and more interested in the men for our last day. I picked out a white top that they could see through, and as soon as we were back on the river, I pulled my bikini top from beneath it.

Not that that mattered so much, since I had a life vest on anyway, but I took it off at lunch.

"Oh yeah, that's better," Paul said and winked at me.

My top was wet and my nipples were tight and clearly visible through it. I was getting looks from the other guys in the tour group too, but I was beyond caring what anyone thought. I was a sex toy for the three men I was with and it was exciting that everyone could probably see that.

The guys were chatting and laughing and I was just sitting with them and not saying much. I was sort of dazed, like usual when I'm around men. Some of the others from the group went for walks, as there was only another hour or so on the river and it was quite early in the afternoon.

Paul checked around, as he had done a few times already. He looked from my nipples to my face, his eyes intense. It seemed like he was going to need another release before tonight, and I was willing to let him if he tried anything with me. Whether he would want my pussy or my mouth, I didn't mind, which I'm sure was in my eyes, judging by the way he was looking at me.

"Would you men like my mouth now and to have me fully tonight?" I asked, peering from Paul to Mario and Foley. "I could suck you off if you want to take me somewhere?"

"Fuck yeah, topless blowjobs, eh guys!" Paul said and checked around again. He was sitting beside me on a log and reached in under my arm, feeling me and thumbing my nipple.

I lifted my arm a little to let him. "If you men don't want to wait until tonight, you could just watch me swallow it this time."

"Aw jeez," Mario groaned and I smiled at him, feeling my blush rise at the thought of swallowing his.

Paul chuckled and squeezed my full breast. "You thirsty, are you, baby? You gonna swallow his as well?"

"Um of course. I know you guys love watching girls do that."

"Yeah we love it alright," Foley said. "Fucking Jared's going to kill me if he ever finds out about this though."

Everyone chuckled. Foley had told them about how he was supposed to be taking care of me. I thought it was fun playing up to that.

"Hmm, well I can't keep a secret, so I hope he doesn't ask me."

Everyone laughed some more. "Oh shit," Foley said.

"Come on, we'd better get this on before everyone gets back," Paul said. He was the leader – the alpha male, and the one that was exciting me so much.

There were several trails into the forest. He led us along one and found a spot that was hidden and the guys would be able to see anyone approaching. Paul put me on my knees and took out his cock. It was already hard. It thrilled me when he forced it into my mouth and held my head in place. I put my hand around it to stop it going down my throat at all because I don't like that.

I just squeezed my eyes shut and sucked as nice as I could until he groaned and held firm, then I opened my eyes and peered up submissively as his cum was pulsing against the back of my mouth and pooling in my closed throat.

"Yeah that's good, baby, you like that?"

"Uh huh." I swallowed and blinked then peered back up. "I liked it."

I more than liked it. It's the best feeling ever – being used by a man. Foley was next and he has some of that dominance in him too. He wound my hair in his hand and held me still while fucking my mouth, snarling down at me.

Paul had only produced a small amount of semen, and Foley did too. Mario was less assertive and needed me to actually suck him off. He took longer, and when he finally bucked and gripped my head, his thick penis throbbed powerfully and his cum absolutely flooded my mouth. Oh my god there was so much of it, making me have to swallow in two big gulps with my eyes watering it tasted so strong.

"Eww yuck!" I scolded, pushing him away and wiping my mouth on the back of my wrist, sniffling and still tearing up while the guys all chuckled.

Foley took my hand and helped me up. I raked back my mussed-up hair. They had pulled up my top and it was bunched above my breasts.

"How about you, baby, your turn yeah?" Paul asked and cuddled me from behind, covering my breasts with both hands and feeling me.

"Um, I can wait until tonight. It's nice for me to just feel you men getting off like that."

"Everyone's heading back," Mario said from looking down the trail. "I think we're heading off."

Paul went ahead with Mario, and Foley held my hand as we followed along behind. I was getting lots of looks from other guys and girls too because my nipples were so visible through my top. Back at camp, I put on my life vest and covered them up. We then paddled out into the current and spent the next hour riding some really great rapids.

The guys were yelling and laughing and just so animated and making my pussy tingle wildly in anticipation of that night.

There was another hour of calm water before we reached the final camp site, where the bus was already parked and waiting. The guys set up our tent away from any others. There was a big barbecue and no limit to the drinks this time. I never drink much and I noticed none of the guys were getting drunk either. They all kept looking over at me as I sat chatting with other people in the group, which was mostly all men around me, with some of the women scowling at me and glaring or rolling eyes disapprovingly.

This too was perfectly normal. I always get on better with the guys at any party and girls all hate me.

It was late by the time I finished making the guys wait to have sex with me. I wanted them to be all crazy and desperate for it and I even flirted with the other men to be sure my three lovers would be all aggressive and ready to take me nice and hard.

It seemed that worked best on Foley because he even shouldered Paul aside to get at me first. He pushed me down and pulled my panties from under my skirt. He pushed up my top and bra, and Paul took them from my arms while Foley entered me and started pounding hard and fast.

"Uh huh," I moaned up at Paul, still holding my wrists.

"Yeah fucking nail the little tease!" he growled at Foley.

That sent tingles rushing all through me and had them filling my belly and tightening into a little ball of ecstasy that just grew and grew until Foley jammed himself hard into me and cried out.

My orgasm hit while he was pumping his cum into me. I writhed and moaned, and he was pulled away and Mario rammed his fat cock into me while Paul kept hold of my wrists. It seemed they were even more worked up than I thought.

"Uh huh like that," I moaned at Mario but his face was stern and he was rolling his fat lower body and humping me. I watched his face until it screwed up in what I can only imagine was some kind of pleasant agony, and he was then pressed hard between my legs and his fat cock was throbbing and no doubt spurting more gooey cum into me.

"Oh yeah that's so tight," he groaned. "That's so fucking hot and tight," he said to me.

"Mmm I can feel you so thick in me, Mario. I love being stretched like this and for a guy to feel me so tight around him."

"Come on, man, my turn," Paul said to his friend. Mario lifted from me and slumped aside. Paul stroked my hair and shifted around beside my head. He supported my neck and surged into my mouth with his erect cock.

"That's it, baby, nice and tight with your soft little hand for me." I gripped as he surged through my fingers. He was on his knees and rolling his hips, spearing through my hand and as far into my throat as I let him.

I supported myself on my side on one elbow. He wound my hair around one hand and kept hold of the back of my neck with the other. He was keeping my head in position and just fucking my hand and mouth with deep slow strokes. He was snarling down at me, absolutely thrilling me. I could feel Foley and Mario's cum seeping from my pussy and all gooey between my thighs, as I had them scissored together and they felt slippery.

This was so perfect though – two sexually sated men watching on with their cum leaking out of me while another dominant man was using my mouth to stimulate and fill his big balls. "Ummm..mmm.." I moaned with my mouth full of cock as my orgasm resurged and thumped through my belly at the mere thought of being taken and used like this.

"Aw fuck yeah!" Paul cried out and thrust hard and held firm, his cock flexing then it began to pulse with powerful bursts of cum slurping into my throat and making me gag.

Jared

"Hi, Bruce, how's it going?"

"Yeah good, Jared, have you heard from Catherine at all. I can't seem to get hold of her."

"No, they would be out of mobile range on the river. Foley said they're back today. Try calling around lunchtime, I reckon. They should be back by then."

"Oh right." Bruce toed at the dirt. He was over his side of our shared back fence. He nodded grimly. "Yeah, I'm sure that's what Catherine said too, now I think about it."

"Hey, she'll be fine, man. Foley's a good guy, he'll be looking after her."

"Yeah I guess… It's just that she's um…" The man swallowed hard, shook his head. "You've noticed, yeah?"

I nodded too. "Yeah, I've noticed. It's hard not to – the way she dresses and that impish bloody smile. It's all tease though, right?"

"Huh, you think!" Bruce scoffed. "I've a feeling there've been quite a few already, both young guys her age and mature men as well."

"Oh shit. How do you um… like, has she confided?"

"Yeah a little. She's just such a free spirit and so damned friendly."

"Right. Yeah. So how do you handle it, Bruce? Are you okay with it?"

"Well how am I supposed to handle it, it's hard enough keeping my own eyes off the girl. I mean, I'm only a step-father. She's not my actual daughter – by blood."

"Oh shit! And um… do you um..?"

Bruce glared. "No, man! Jesus, I'm just saying I don't know where to look half the time around the house. I'd never dream of touching the girl, for christ's sake. I love her mother and I wouldn't dream of touching *any* other woman!"

"Yeah, yeah, sure. Of course. Sorry, man, I didn't mean anything," I apologised quickly.

My neighbour cocked one eyebrow at me. "And you haven't either, right?"

I felt my neck and face go red. "Me? No! Hell no!.. I mean, I wouldn't, man. There's no way!"

Bruce left me with a dismissive wave and went back inside. I was in my study at the front of the house later that afternoon when I saw Foley's 4WD pull up on the road and Catherine got out with her backpack, Foley taking off and not stopping in at all. Bruce met Catherine on their front veranda and greeted her with a hug, taking her pack and ushering her inside before craning his neck to look up the street where Foley's car had gone.

The girl absolutely intrigued me and had been doing so since she was a young teen developing her womanly wiles. I saw her later that afternoon hanging washing in a short dress that flashed her little pink panties every time she raised her arms to peg an item of clothing on the line.

I wondered if Foley had fucked her. I had my binoculars out and was examining her crotch as I considered that. I couldn't tell of course, but the image was in my head now and I was feeling my semi-erect cock while playing it out.

The girl next door went back inside and I opened my favourite porn site and finished off. I was early thirties and single. I often made do masturbating rather than dating, although I'd been quite active socially of late.

I never heard from Foley and didn't chase him up. Over the next little while I kept an eye on Catherine and often chatted with Bruce about what she was up to. She was going out all the time and would occasionally stay over at a girlfriend's house. She spent a few months seeing some weird older guy, but soon broke that off, much to Bruce's relief, and mine, as her make-believe big brother.

One weekend about six months after the canoeing trip, I heard Foley was back in town after spending a while on the road with his sales job. He was staying at a local hotel and Bruce told me Catherine was to be meeting him for dinner. Just for fun, I invited myself along and crashed their party, finding them at the bar of the hotel restaurant having pre-dinner drinks.

"Well imagine bumping into you pair here!" I declared, feigning total surprise.

Foley

"Settle down a bit would you – you little tart? He's not stupid. He'll pick up on what's going on!"

We were up in my room having an after dinner drink or two. Jared had gone to the toilet, and Catherine was grinning over cheekily. "I don't care anymore," she said flatly.

"You don't care?"

She slithered over to where I was sitting on a chair I'd pulled from the dining table. She straddled me with her little black party dress bunching up around her waist. "Nope! Don't care at all," she teased and kissed me on the lips.

"Yeah right! He'd freak and you know it," I challenged, kissing her back but listening intently for the toilet flush.

"Well, I'm not leaving without getting a you-know-what tonight, so what are we going to do?" Her lips were warm and soft, her perfume intoxicating.

I had a plan. "I say we go back down to the bar. You leave and sneak back here, and I'll wait a little while and call it a night."

The toilet flushed, and I pushed the little slut off my lap. She clung on giggling until we nearly got caught, then she jumped back onto the sofa with her legs tucked up and her panties on display. Jared's eyes flashed to them then settled on mine as he sat beside Catherine. I couldn't help glancing down, but I wrenched my eyes back up to meet my friend's.

There was weirdness!

"So, that wasn't a bad feed, was it?" I said, trying to get the conversation fired up again real quick.

Jared burped and patted his gut. He was a heavily built guy and could actually kill me quite easily, I expected. "Yeah I'm stuffed," he offered.

"Serves you right," Catherine shot at him. "Yours, half of mine and two desserts!"

He grinned at her. "Can't let good food go to waste."

"Ever?" she teased, poking his belly. "Gosh, when are you due?"

Jared came back with something about Catherine still being skin and bones, and he showed her how easily he could hold her two wrists in one hand while he tickled her. I was sitting there across from them checking out her little panties and kind of glancing away whenever Jared looked up. I was also having issues with a burgeoning erection over the fact that Catherine had declared she wasn't leaving without a fuck.

She was extremely ticklish and was squirming and laughing hysterically. Jared kept it up, digging into her ribs and clutching her knees. He had her pushing with her feet, and her little dress had bunched right up again with her panties showing. He kept at her though, and when he finally relented, her shoulder straps were hanging down and one side of her dress had slipped, exposing a breast.

Jared still held her wrists, and she was red in the face and half choking from all the laughing. Her chest was heaving, and she fought to catch her breath.

Jared chuckled, glancing at her breast and releasing her wrists. "Oops!"

"Bully!" she shot back at him and punched his arm. She glanced down at her breast too, then she quite strangely just rubbed her wrists – first one then the other – and as yet she hadn't covered herself. Jared was just staring at her boob, and she glanced down again then finally lifted her shoulder strap into place.

"So, what ever happened with Tom?" Jared asked her.

"Tom just didn't work out. He was nice at first, though."

"Someone said he was into swing clubs and stuff," Jared went on. "Is that true?"

Catherine's colour had returned to normal, but she blushed red that time. "Who told you that?"

"Tracy, I think."

"Oh. Well, she told me you're hot, so what would she know?" Catherine finally tugged her dress down. Her panties had still been on display until then.

"Tom was a bit of a loser, though, wasn't he?" Foley tossed in.

"No, he was really nice but he was actually gay. He was always getting with the bi guys at the clubs."

Jared's eyebrows lifted.

Catherine blushed again. "Yes, we did go to swinger parties," she declared defiantly. "If you must know!"

Jared grinned. "What was that like?"

Catherine looked from Jared to me and back again. "It was fun mostly."

"Ever get with more than one guy?" Jared went on. He seemed strangely relaxed and openly interested.

Catherine was on her knees on the sofa fixing her long blond hair with a clip that had come loose while thrashing around before. She sat back with her legs tucked up again, and that time they were swayed towards Jared. She eyed him curiously. "Promise not to tell my dad?"

Jared shrugged. "Yeah, of course!"

She blushed a little again. "Then yes, I've been with more than one guy."

She took in both of us men, looking back and forth. "Some of the parties got pretty wild actually, and there was always more guys than girls."

Jared nodded and was thoughtful for a moment. "I've been with two women," he stated. "And with a woman and another guy," he added, smiling over at me.

I didn't know what to make of that and just frowned.

"Who were the two girls?" Catherine asked with interest. Her shoulder strap had slipped again and the top part of one breast was visible.

"Tracy and Tamara," Jared said. "It was some show they put on, too!"

"Oh my gosh! Tamara?"

"And what's with this other guy deal?" I asked my buddy. "You don't mean..?"

Jared shrugged and sort of nodded. "Yeah, I've tried it a couple of times. Not with just a guy. With a woman as well, I can get into it."

"Oh shit!" I was picturing my buddy with another dude right then, and talk about weirdness!

"That's so cool," Catherine said to Jared. "I would never have guessed you'd be that open minded."

"Yeah, well, it sort of just happened the first time," he explained, seemingly glad to get it out there.

Catherine was grinning, and she glanced across at me before she announced, "So, me and Foley have done it."

Jared looked at me. "When?" he asked flatly.

"When we went rafting and a few times since," Catherine answered.

Jared then smiled. "Well, that's all right, then. As long as it wasn't back when you were under age." Then he grabbed Catherine and tickled her again. "You little tart, wait till I tell your dad." He had her wriggling and thrashing about, and he kept it up until she was totally red-faced and panting, and he left her with her dress up around her waist and one breast bare again.

She sat there like that and gulped down the last of her rum and coke before she could talk. Then she handed me the empty. "Another one, please?" Then she punched Jared's arm and made him laugh.

"I think we should have a game of Euchre," Jared said. "That's how I ended up trying it."

"Trying what?" I asked, handing Catherine her drink and sitting back down. She had just glanced from her breast up to Jared, and she fixed her shoulder strap, blushing a little.

"That's how I ended up trying my first blowjob," Jared said. "Simple rules! We play one game with all three of us, and the winner gets oral from whomever they choose. Then the remaining two play a second game, and the winner gets oral from whomever they choose! The loser misses out."

"Okay, I'm in!" Catherine declared immediately.

I laughed. "No fucking way!"

Jared sort of shrugged. "Yeah, you're probably right. I guess it's getting a bit late and I should be taking my little sister home."

Catherine turned on me. "Come on, let's play. Please?"

"Yeah, and what if *he* wins?" I protested. "Fuck, are you serious, Jared? You really gave a dude a blowjob?"

Jared just smiled. "What, and you've never wondered what it'd be like?"

Well, actually I *had* wondered, but there's no way I was going to confess to it. I had an idea, though. Jared wasn't that good at euchre, and if he won I could always back out, anyway. And if I won, it would be fun to get a blowjob from Catherine while my protective buddy watched.

I looked at Catherine. "Fine then. Let's play!"

*

I always had a deck of cards in my bag when travelling, and after pushing the furniture back we sat around on the floor, and I dealt.

"Make it first to five," Catherine said. I can't wait a whole game.

We played a few hands where Catherine and I won a point each. Then Jared picked up two points for a euchre, and that was the only hand he won before Catherine hit five points and squealed with glee.

"I pick you," she said to me, and she lifted to the sofa and guided me between her legs.

I kissed her knee and glanced back at Jared, checking with him. Jared sat up on a chair and gave another little shrug and nod.

Catherine wiggled down until she was sitting right on the edge of the sofa with her legs slightly apart. I kissed my way along her inner-thigh and tugged her skirt up. Then I kissed her pussy through her little panties, and she ground her hips and moaned. I could smell how wet she was already. "Do you want me to take these off?" I asked her, nuzzling and kissing into her heat again.

She looked over at Jared, and I glanced back to see my buddy's face kind of blank as he sat there watching. "Okay," Catherine said to me, and she lifted so I could pull off her panties. She giggled over at Jared. "You'd better not tell, though."

Jared met her eyes and smiled. He then looked back down at her legs as I was opening them. Catherine just blushed and watched his face.

I could see her juices glistening from her reddened inner-folds as I kissed her thighs and worked my fingers in, massaging and spreading her legs even wider before drawing the scent of her arousal then slicing my tongue into her. She was hot and slippery, and I probed deep for a moment and tasted her sweet, tangy juices. I licked tenderly. Her clit was swollen and ripe, but I avoided contact with it and merely opened her outer folds and sliced the tip of my tongue through the soft pink flesh.

Catherine's hips rolled, forcing more contact, but I moved with her and sucked a delicate fold of tissue into my mouth and held it. She groaned and her body convulsed, and I felt the weight of her hand against the back of my head as I sunk my tongue into her dripping little gash and searched deep inside of her again. Then her body tensed and shuddered once more as I sliced my tongue up through her slit, and with the firm tip of it, I started massaging her clit.

Catherine's legs splayed as she ground her opening against my face. I felt into her with my middle finger, and she moaned and clung to my head. I swallowed the juices oozing into my mouth and licked and sucked while working my finger in and out of her hot little hole. I was sucking again on her swollen clit when she erupted into orgasm. I could feel her searing inner walls clamp around my finger, and I waited for her contractions to subside before gently removing it.

Catherine was lying back with her legs spread wide and her chest heaving while I sat up and wiped my chin on my arm. She was watching Jared's face again, and he was just staring at her swollen pussy.

She closed her legs and he glanced up, so she smiled shyly. Then his eyes lowered, and she opened her legs again but squirmed her hands between them and covered herself, her shoulder straps sliding down to her elbows and uncovering her breasts. They were both completely exposed, and she looked up from them to meet Jared's smile again.

"Nice," he said.

"Thank you."

He looked back down at her legs. She moved her hands, rubbing her inner thighs and letting him look at her pussy. She was biting her lip when he peered up again. "Hmm, that looks very inviting, little sister." Catherine's blush deepened, and she pressed her thighs together with her hands wedged between.

Jared shuffled the cards. He grinned at me. "All right then. Down to you and me."

"Or we could just call it and we could see you tomorrow," I said to him, but he was already dealing.

Catherine giggled. "No, you have to play."

She wound her panties around a wrist and sat on the floor, her legs bent to the side with one back a bit and her cunt on display. She tugged her dress up but didn't fix the shoulder straps, leaving the garment just clinging to her firm little nipples. Each time Catherine would move or raise her glass to drink, her dress would slip and reveal a bare breast again, and she would casually fix it. I played distractedly and noticed Jared looking as well. Jared also got the run of the cards and made it to five pretty quickly.

"There's no way I'm doin' it," I said flatly. "No fucking way in the world!"

Jared just smiled, still so cool and in control. "That's fine. I pick Catherine, anyway," he said, turning to her.

She blushed fully.

"Is that alright?" he asked her.

My dick lifted immediately.

"Um, I don't know," Catherine uttered. "But I thought you were going to make him!"

"There's no fucking way I would have," I stated. "And I'd have picked you too if I won, in case anyone's wondering."

Jared grinned over at me. "There's no way I'd do it with you either. That'd be too weird!"

"Oh, and making *me* do it isn't weird?" Catherine asked. She was smiling, though, and seemed playful enough to perhaps do it. Jared released his erect penis, and she slapped her hand over her mouth, giggling while her eyes bulged focusing on it.

He chuckled. "Don't worry, doesn't bite. It's just like any other man's dick."

"Hmm, I suppose," Catherine said, shaking her head in defeat. "It's ending up with a mouthful of what's inside of those that's the big problem though," she added. Jared had worked his balls out through the fly of his trousers. They were quite large. "Well, I guess it's only semen. Although, it's going to feel like doing it for my brother!"

Jared just smiled down at her. "Come on then, little sister."

Catherine giggled and blushed a bit deeper. "But you can't watch! You have to wear a blindfold, otherwise I'll chicken out halfway through."

I pulled off my tie and tossed it to Jared.

"And what are you grinning at?" Catherine shot at me.

"Nothin'!" I declared innocently. "Do you want some help?"

Jared was blindfolded and ready to start.

"How about you take him in your mouth and I'll help rock you back and forth?" I suggested, getting down on my knees and taking Catherine's hips as she squirmed back against me.

"Are you gonna fuck my little sis?" Jared asked.

I chuckled back. "Yeah, we're gonna spit-roast her."

Catherine slapped my arm. "You guys have been planning this, haven't you?" she accused.

"No, but always fantasized about it," Jared confessed quite seriously.

Catherine was kneeling in front of Jared, and I slipped into her from behind and made her moan a little as she ground back onto my dick. "Have you really fantasized about this?" she asked Jared, closing her hand around his erection.

"Yeah, only about a million times since you started filling out your bikini," he groaned, and he held her shoulder and tried to thrust upward towards her face.

"Well, you can seriously never tell anyone I did it," she uttered. "I'd die if my parents ever found out I sucked you off."

She was stroking him a little bit, and I rocked back then thrust forward as she opened her lips over the head of her childhood friend's cock and kissed it. "I can't believe I'm going to do this," she said softly, and she took the head into her mouth and sucked it. And as she did that I started slow fucking her with long, deep strokes.

Catherine kept her eyes closed and kept Jared's dick in her mouth. He was thrusting as well, both of us surging into her at the same time. She braced back against me and held Jared's thighs, letting him fuck her mouth. We went at her like that for a while before she lifted her head, gasping for breath, and she held Jared's flexing cock to the side, peering up at him. "No peeking!" she scolded playfully. "I won't let you cum in my mouth if you're watching me."

"Wouldn't be the same if you only stroke me off," he said to her.

"Well, it wouldn't be the same for me either," she went on teasingly, and she kept his dick to one side and sucked on his balls. "I want to taste what's in these but not if you're peeking!"

I ejaculated right then. I ground hard into her and bucked, and she moaned over the cock she had taken back into her mouth while I emptied my balls inside of her.

Jared took hold of her head and started fucking her mouth again. She mostly kept her eyes closed, but she would glance up at his face and check he wasn't looking sometimes. He wasn't that big, so she could take most of him in, though his last little bit of thrust made her throat swell and the veins in her neck expand.

She held his thigh and let him control the depth until he started losing it and surging towards his climax, then she gripped the base of his dick while he bucked and held firm. Then her eyes shot open in surprise, and she frowned a little as his balls clenched and he started ejaculating in her mouth.

She held him there and kept the head of his dick inserted beyond her lips while his shaft flexed with each spurt of cum. It went on for a long time, Catherine's eyes widening as she softly sucked the last of it. "Damn that's a lot," she then mumbled, giggling awkwardly with her mouth still full.

Jared pulled off the blindfold and remained slumped back gasping for breath. He grinned at her. She shook her head, smiling with her lips closed and her mouth obviously still full.

"Show us," I said, and Catherine rolled her eyes at us both and opened her mouth. She was holding a pool of very thick, white and stringy fluid. It oozed up over her tongue and lower teeth, and her eyes watered a little as she closed her mouth again.

"You gonna swallow or spit?" I teased, positioning her back on the floor.

She shook her head again, blushing. Then her eyes softly closed as she swallowed and frowned at the taste. "I can't believe how much there was," she scolded, slapping Jared's leg. "Next time don't hold back so much!"

"Next time?" Jared grinned. "Is there going to be a next time?"

Catherine blushed again.

"I don't know – maybe," she said as I lay down on top of her and worked my renewed erection back into her. "But only if you don't tell," she uttered, peering up at Jared again and making him look up from her bare breasts.

"I might even start doing that for you whenever we're both home if you don't tell," she added sweetly. "If we could just sneak when Daddy doesn't know."

I surged into her hot cunt. "Haha, regular blowjobs from the girl next door, eh Jared..!"

He got down on his knees and smoothed her hair aside, lifted her head a little and fed his cock back into her mouth. "Ooh yeah, getting sucked off by the girl next door when her daddy doesn't know... Perfect!"

** The End **

Just with your Fingers

Catherine

I had drifted out of the conversation and was sitting on the hotel room couch watching my boyfriend Tom and ex-sort-of-boyfriend Foley chatting and laughing over their drinks. They were seated at the bar, which was full-sized and fully stocked. The hotel room was really beautiful – a luxury suite in black leather, chrome and marble.

Tom and Foley got on well, Foley having introduced me to Tom before vanishing on one of his sales trips and being gone for the past few months. Foley was a cute surfer type with scruffy blond hair and amazing blue eyes. Tom was kind of tall and lithe, not very sporty at all but quite the intellectual, and attractive in that way.

The thing about Tom though, was his proclivities. Foley introduced us at a swinger party. Tom was a friend of the host and kind of an extra male, as he was there alone. Foley had taken me to two swinger parties, but we were never that serious and not technically a couple, so arguably not actually swinging either.

After dating Tom for a month though, he wanted to try swinging for real. He took me back to the same venue, which was a small private group. And after three or four times getting with other couples, he revealed what his actual proclivity was.

It was well into this particular evening and I was a little bit drunk. The two other visiting couples had gone home, leaving only the host couple and this one other single guy. I was in the living room with the woman, Blanche. I had already had sex with one of the men who had gone home. Blanche's husband, Hudson, was up the hallway leaning against an open bedroom doorway. He had been chatting with Tom and this other single guy, whose name I never caught, but the conversation had faded and I could hear strange sounds coming from that bedroom. They were kind of deep sounding squeals and whimpers. I was curious.

"Go on, sweetie," Blanch encouraged, smiling knowingly, and just then her husband looked to me and motioned for me to come have a look too.

The squealing whimpers were accompanied by a bed squeaking. My body flushed with curious excitement as I approached.

"Oh fuck yeah, take it, man," this fit looking personal trainer guy growled, and as I peeped around the open doorway I saw him thump against Tom's bottom.

Tom was on his knees and elbows, gripping a pillow and whimpering into it. This other guy was holding his hips and fucking him. I was shocked and intrigued.

The guy pulled back and all the way out. He gripped his cock and slapped my boyfriend's arse with it. He looked over at us. "You up?" he asked Hudson.

"Na, man, keep going, I'll have him when you're done."

I met and held Tom's gaze. He was blushing embarrassingly. I was just glaring, completely stunned.

The trainer guy had a huge dick, both long and thick. It was way too big for anal, surely! Though I'd never tried anal myself. It just looked way big, an as he entered Tom again, Tom's eyes bulged and he whimpered into the pillow again.

The guy fucking him gripped the back of his neck and settled into a steady rhythm, pulling back about half way then surging all the way into my boyfriend's arse and grinding against him, snarling and smirking at Tom's girlish whimper.

The older man, Hudson, was feeling his cock too now. He had approached the end of the bed, with Tom's bulging eyes rolling back to watch him getting ready for his turn. The woman, Blanche, was behind me and squeezing the back of my neck, her face at my shoulder.

The muscular personal trainer guy let out a deep growl and jammed himself hard against my whimpering boyfriend's bottom. He was inside Tom unprotected and obviously cumming.

"Mmm, do you like that?" Blanche asked into my ear.

"Uh huh it's amazing. I've never seen two men doing it before."

The trainer guy pulled out of my boyfriend's arse and the older man knelt behind with a smaller cock in his fist and positioned the head. Tom shifted his knees apart and lowered a bit to help this other man, who was kind of short and stocky.

"Nyaa..ahh…" Tom groaned as the man thumped against his bottom, and I watched fascinated again while my suddenly-less-appealing boyfriend was fucked and cum inside for a second time.

*

I was flushing hot as I sipped my wine and watched Tom laughing with Foley – remembering that first time I'd seen Tom with another man. That was a month ago, and we've been back to the swinger group twice since then, with Tom getting with men on both of those nights too.

We talked after that first time and I was fine with it. I have no problem with men being gay or bisexual. I get on great with gay men and women.

Something definitely changed for me with regard to Tom though. I was thinking about it again as I watched him there across the room at the bar. It wasn't any kind of disrespect or anything like that. He was still a man with me and could be quite dominant – equally as dominant as the other men were with him.

No, it wasn't that I had stopped seeing him as a strong man. He glanced over at me and I smiled. *No, I think it's a matter of me being jealous of him!*

Oh my god I just reasoned that for the first time and it all made perfect sense. I was jealous of the other men wanting to fuck him and not me.

My boyfriend has become my competition!

That realization flooded through me as he approached and leant down to kiss me. "Are you okay, love?"

I blushed, my mind whirling.

Foley

"I don't think I can go through with this," Catherine said softly as she wrung her hands in her lap and peered up at her boyfriend.

She was sitting there on the fine leather sofa of a hotel room we had followed a complete stranger to. Her slender, lightly tanned thighs were virtually trembling. Tom glanced in the direction of the door where the guy we had met was about due to return. He turned back to Catherine and shrugged.

"I was okay down in the bar, but I don't think I want to now," Catherine went on, including me in her plea.

I touched her shoulder and smiled, attempting to support her, but as her hand closed over mine her little top gaped and exposed a nipple through the lace of her bra. I was leaning from over the back of the sofa, and I rested there gently massaging as we discussed the situation. Her hand had slipped back into her lap, but with the action of my thumb upon her shoulder I was able to work the fabric of her little top to gape enough that I could see her nipple again.

"So, the whole idea's off, then?" Tom challenged, though he seemed relieved. I had more or less talked him into offering Catherine to this particular guy.

She half shrugged. "Well, not the whole idea. I'll still... you know... if we go home, I'll still let Foley."

"Let me what?" I grinned down at her, and she blushed as she glanced up at me. It had been six months since I had taken Catherine white-water rafting and first gotten lucky with her. It had been two months since I had last seen her and Tom.

"What are we going to tell this guy then?" Tom went on nervously.

"Are you sure you don't want to?" I asked Catherine, and I reached further down into her top and softly pinched her nipple. Her hand closed over my wrist, but it only rested there. "I was kinda looking forward to watching him fuck you," I whispered into her hair, and her cheeks reddened again. "Watching you take this off and showing him these nice little titties. And watching while you lifted up that little skirt and spread your legs for him," I went on, feeling her neck quiver as I breathed against it.

"He should be back soon. If they didn't have any in the hotel, there was that shop across the street," Tom stammered, glancing back over his shoulder, then his eyes returned to Catherine's chest.

"Do you like this?" I asked, still softly rolling her nipple.

She looked up at her boyfriend, her eyes closing then slowly opening again, and her bottom lip curling beneath her teeth as her body arched against my hand.

"Think she's coming around," I said to Tom.

He offered a nervous smile.

"How about you pull her panties down," I suggested. "Don't lift her skirt though, just reach up under it and take them off her." Then I sucked on Catherine's neck as her boyfriend knelt before her.

Tom didn't look up. He wiped his brow on his sleeve then reached under her skirt. I could feel Catherine's heart pounding through her breast as her panties were worked from beneath her hips and peeled down her thighs.

"I'm still not sure about this," she uttered, clinging to my arm as her underwear was carefully removed from her feet.

Tom moved back and leant against the chair opposite. His eyes never lifted, and he sat staring at his girlfriend's legs. Her panties were clutched in his hand as he wiped his brow on his sleeve again.

"Unsure is okay," I whispered into Catherine's ear. "Letting a complete stranger take you right in front of your boyfriend is always gonna feel a bit uneasy, but imagine how it's gonna feel when he's got that big fat cock up you! I saw it in the toilet, you know? It's a monster!"

"Shut up!" Catherine chuckled, pushing my head away.

"No, I'm serious! Hope they've got super-size at the shop." I nibbled my way back along her shoulder until her head tilted to give me access to her neck once more.

"Have you ever had one of those big porno movie cocks before?"

"Um – maybe? But this man feels aggressive, and I'm not sure I want to do this with him."

"He won't hurt you or anything," I assured.

"No, I don't mean like that," Catherine uttered. "He just seems really pushy and sort of arrogant."

Catherine looked to Tom, and he glanced back up at her. "Up to you," he said shakily.

"Do you still want me to?" she asked in reply.

"Yeah, I guess," Tom answered, and Catherine blushed again.

"And you?" she asked me.

"Hell yeah! I'd like to watch him doing ya," I said softly as I slipped my fingers inside the cup of her bra for the first time. Her chest lifted as she caught a breath. Her tit was warm and soft, and I massaged it firmly. Her hands slipped between her knees, which clamped together as her body arched up. "Open your legs while I do this," I breathed into her neck. "Show your boyfriend what this other guy's getting," I went on, and as I touched her arm her knees parted and Tom's eyes lowered and set. His face was ashen, his expression blank. Catherine's hands pressed into her inner thighs. Her legs opened and stretched her skirt causing it to roll and gather upward.

"Fuck me!" Tom groaned.

"Is it wet?" I asked, but Tom didn't answer, so I moved back to Catherine's ear. "Is it?" I whispered, slipping my other hand down her top and under her bra to cover her right breast. It was the first time I'd touched that one, and she moaned softly as her hands pressed up beneath her skirt, her body arching and her legs spreading wider. "Is it ready for that guy's big hard cock?" I went on lewdly.

"Uh huh," Catherine moaned, her mouth opening as I kissed her.

I kissed her passionately. I had a nipple between each thumb and forefinger, and I rolled them, gently pulling on them while searching her hot mouth with my tongue. The door opened, and the guy we were waiting for, Brad, sauntered in and slowly approached to stand beside Tom. Catherine broke away from my kiss and wiped her mouth on her hand as she peered up at the guy. She had closed her legs.

"Sorry I took so long. Hope I didn't miss anything," he said with a smile.

"We were just gettin' her warmed up," I answered.

Tom lifted himself up onto the chair and held his girlfriend's gaze for a moment before her eyes lowered, and she nervously rubbed at the hem of her skirt. I slipped around and claimed the other chair, leaving her alone on the sofa.

Brad motioned to the seat beside Catherine, and Tom nodded, so he sat down. She glanced up and offered him a little smile but quickly looked away. "Everything still a go?" he asked us other two men.

"Yeah, except Catherine said we had to watch. Hope you don't mind?" I replied.

"I did not!" Catherine complained, smiling through her embarrassment, and she tossed a cushion at me.

I laughed. "Well, not exactly, I suppose. But we're watching anyway!"

"Right here okay?" Brad asked, lightly touching Catherine's arm with the back of his fingers.

She visibly flinched, and her face reddened further as her eyes sought her boyfriend. Brad's hand moved slowly, and gently stroked up and down, then he reached a little further and cupped her right breast. Her nipple was already firm and poking at the thin fabric covering it. He softly squeezed it.

Catherine's eyes turned to me then moved back to Tom as she kept nervously fiddling. Brad watched her face. He was sitting sideways, facing her. His free hand closed over the bulge in his trousers, the action causing Catherine's head to turn.

"Did you get condoms?" Tom suddenly blurted.

"In the pocket," Brad answered, nodding in the direction of the coat he'd placed on the back of Tom's chair.

"Shame about that though, yeah?" I ventured. "I mean, waste of a perfectly good load of cum when it doesn't end up inside a girl."

"A perfectly good load," Brad echoed, causing Catherine to blush and smile again.

"Well, it's alright for you men, but I'm the one who'd have to worry all month!" she complained.

"So you're in danger of getting pregnant if we cum in you?" I asked, touching Catherine's knee with my foot.

She moved as if to prevent it but allowed me to move her leg a little, although only for a moment before closing them. "I don't know. I should be okay right now but I'm not a hundred percent sure," she answered, peering from me to Brad.

Brad edged closer and lifted his arm to the back of the sofa as he leaned against her. He'd been casually fondling her breast up until then, and while Tom and I watched, he reached under her top, and we could see his hand close over her more forcefully.

Catherine looked down at her chest. Her hands had been together in her lap, but they moved, with her arms falling aside and her chest lifting.

"She's got nice little tits," Brad said to Tom, and Catherine looked to her boyfriend too, blushing again.

I grinned. "Are you under her bra?"

"Yeah, I've got it pulled up over them," Brad said, returning a grin. "Nothing like bare tits with tight little nipples."

"Mmm but not too rough," Catherine uttered, with her eyes closing as she arched back in the sofa, and Brad's hand slipped from under her top and touched the side of her skirt. She twisted an arm around behind and undid her bra. He helped her unthread it out from her top and drop it on the floor. I scooped it up and held it to my nose.

"Let's pull this up a bit, okay?" Brad said. "Just up over your hips so we can see," he went on, and Catherine lifted while he tugged at her skirt, gathering it from beneath her bottom and pulling it all the way up to her belly. "Yeah! Now that's fucking nice!" the guy groaned, smoothing over the tiny patch of hair and causing Catherine's body to lift again. But he only touched her briefly with his fingertips, then his hand went back up under her top.

Catherine's fingers were pressing into the leather sofa, and her knees were holding together, but her slender thighs didn't meet. We could all see that the smooth, slightly puffy lips of her slit were pink and moist.

"So, you guys do her regularly?" Brad ventured.

"Well, he does, I guess. But no, I only flew in this afternoon and had no idea I'd be getting lucky," I explained.

"You haven't fucked her yet then?" Brad went on.

"Yeah, I've fucked her a few times but not lately. But I've got all weekend and I'll be getting a few loads off in her, for sure, dude."

"Oh really *for sure*?" Catherine challenged playfully. "And what if I decide you have to use condoms?"

"Well – I guess. But it's part of the excitement, isn't it, Tom? Having her walk round all weekend with another man's cum in her panties."

"Or maybe without the panties." Tom smiled, and Catherine held his gaze with her cheeks reddening a little again. "But only if she decides it's safe," he added more seriously.

Catherine peered around at the three of us. "I don't see what the fuss is about. I'm sure you men can't even feel when you're wearing a condom. As long as you're inside me when you cum, it's going to feel the same, isn't it?"

"True, but not the point," Brad offered thoughtfully. "For me, it's knowing when you pull out you leave the girl with your load. I mean, that's what it's all about, right?"

"Yeah – full lube service with insemination," I added, and Catherine just shook her head and rolled her eyes.

We all chuckled, but Brad went on to speak more seriously. He addressed Catherine and included Tom. "So, it should be fine, but there's some chance of getting you pregnant, yeah?"

"Yes," Catherine replied. "I'm not on birth control at the moment."

Brad addressed Tom. "So, that makes it that little bit more exciting for you as the cuckold, eh? With your woman fertile, and I know I'm fully fertile. Would you like Catherine to choose not to use rubbers?"

Tom blushed. "Guess I wouldn't mind," he answered meekly, looking to Catherine.

"Yeah, that's sexy," Brad went on easily. "And you get to watch me fuck her too." He groped Catherine's tits lewdly. "You getting wet, baby?"

"Uh huh," Catherine uttered. "I'm getting wet for him, not for you," she said to her boyfriend.

Tom looked at her pussy then peered back up, his face still red from embarrassment.

"And if I let them cum inside me, you still have to use condoms, okay?" Catherine went on.

Tom nodded. "Okay." He looked to Brad and me and got up. "I'm going out for a smoke."

"You can smoke in here," Brad offered.

"No, Catherine doesn't like it. I'll only be a few minutes."

"Is everything okay?" Catherine asked him, a little concerned and pulling at the hem of her skirt.

"Yeah, everything's fine. You know how I am after an hour without a puff. But don't get too carried away while I'm gone, yeah?"

*

Brad got up and went to the bar after Tom left. "What'll ya have?" he called back, and Catherine asked for wine while I agreed to a beer.

Catherine stood and fixed her hair. "What happened to my panties?"

"I think Tom put them in your handbag," I suggested, shrugging.

Brad placed the drinks on a coffee table beside the sofa. "Why? You don't need them, do you?"

"No, I didn't want to lose them."

"Your bra's with him. And I can get at your tits easier."

Catherine's blush deepened again. "Foley, hand it over."

She was standing before the two of us men. Her eyes averted as she reached over grabbing her bra, folding it and placing it with her handbag.

"Wait!" Brad called to her. "How about bending over a bit further so we can have a look at you from behind like that?"

"No!" Catherine cried, blushing furiously. "Don't be crude!"

"It's not crude. Just want a bit of a look is all, don't we?" Brad appealed to me.

"Yeah, that'd be nice," I suggested, grinning hopefully up at Catherine.

She smiled through her blush, glancing away and shaking her head. "So, what exactly do you want me to do?"

"Just come over for a minute," Brad replied, standing and gesturing with his hand, and Catherine approached tentatively. "We just wanna see how that shaved little slit opens up when you bend over," he went on, leaning her forward over the sofa.

I stood, and Catherine peered back at the guy as he approached. Brad lifted her skirt and bent down to inspect her. He touched the back of her thighs and squeezed, peeling the lips of her pussy open. Her inner folds were tacky, and using his thumbs, he opened them wider.

I looked to Catherine. "Are you okay?" I asked her sincerely, but as I did, Brad sliced the tip of his tongue through her open slit.

"Mmm.. huhh," Catherine whimpered.

Brad held her open and continued licking, just slowly and without penetrating. He was teasing the folds of her labia, then his middle finger appeared from beneath his tongue, and he forced it all the way in.

Catherine's breath caught and her head dropped to her arm as she squirmed back. The guy's probing searched higher, and he peeled the cheeks of her bottom open with his other hand while trying to insert the tip of his tongue into her little hole and slowly fucking her with his finger.

I watched for a few minutes, just touching Catherine's back and gently massaging. "Do you wanna have a go?" Brad asked me, standing and stepping aside.

Catherine watched as I moved around behind her. "This okay?" I asked, and she nodded, then I poked the tip of my middle finger in and inserted it all the way up her.

Brad felt under her top, groping her tits. "Tight, isn't she?"

She looked to him then peered back over her shoulder at me.

"Like that?" I said to her, rubbing the tip of my index finger over her clit, and her eyes closed and her body arched backward, so I kept at it, vibrating my hand against her and pumping my middle finger in and out slowly while maintaining pressure on her clit.

"Yeah, she's gonna cum!" Brad said. He'd lifted her and had both hands under her top. "Cum for us, baby!" he groaned, and her hands went to his head as he ate into her neck. I continued finger fucking her until suddenly her vaginal walls contracted, then I stopped and held firmly up her, keeping the pressure on her little button.

"Aah, keep going like that. HUHH," Catherine's entire body tensed and started to tremble softly. Brad kept hold of her tits and continued sucking on her neck. I waited until her vaginal walls released before carefully withdrawing my finger. It had all been a bit restrained, but Brad and I smiled to each other while we fixed

Catherine's clothing back into place and steadied her upright.

"Was that good?" Brad asked her with a grin. And he offered her drink.

She didn't respond but smiled, sipping the mouthful of wine he passed her, fanning her face, which was quite red.

"And the wine – okay?"

"Yes, it's fine thanks."

"That's good. I'll get another bottle sent up. That was the last of it."

Brad left for the bedroom where the phone was. Catherine sat down and finally met my eyes.

"Been wanting to do that since I first saw you at Jared's place after school one day," I said, sort of measured. It was true that I'd fantasized about fingering her that day.

"You had been wanting to do what? To finger me?" Catherine asked, a little awkwardly.

"Well, yeah. It's what we used to do back then, remember?"

She giggled. "Yes, but not quite like that."

"And you liked it from behind?"

"Yeah, I did. And the other ways too."

"Well, I might have to finger you a few more times to work that out," I tried, earning a little smile and blush.

"But you really have to promise not to tell anyone about this. It still feels strange with you being Jared's friend."

"Yeah, but he won't find out."

Jared was her neighbour and like a big brother to her.

"Find out what?" Brad asked as he returned from the bedroom.

"I don't know, find out what happened to Tom, I suppose. How many smokes is he having?"

"No, I saw him out the window. He's downstairs talking to some people. He had a beer 'n that. I think he might be a while."

Catherine smiled up at Brad. "And what about my wine? I'm so thirsty."

"Yeah, it's on its way. Room service had finished but Reg is running up with it for you."

"Who's Reg?"

"One of the doormen. He was just doing a luggage run or something, then he was gonna get it."

"Is he old and wrinkly by any chance?" I asked.

"Old and wrinkly? Yeah, I guess you could say that. Why?"

"Well, I just remembered Catherine was saying how much she likes old wrinkly guys."

"Lol, how much I like vomiting on them," Catherine shot back immediately.

"Well, he wouldn't appreciate that, but he'd probably enjoy a little up-skirt peep," Brad suggested playfully, warming to the tease and moving closer to Catherine.

"No, he wouldn't. It's just your dirty minds," Catherine protested.

"No, seriously! I know him well, and he's always checking out the ladies."

"So, he's a dirty old man, then?"

"Sure he is," Brad said, stroking hair from Catherine's face. "And yeah he'd probably get a thrill out of a little flash. But who cares about him? I'm just thinking how it'd be if he saw you sitting here with two men and your cunt on display. You do wanna show it to us again, don't you?"

"Yes, I do, but I'm a bit nervous about some old guy coming in and seeing me like that."

"Well, when he knocks on the door, if you feel uncomfortable we'll just forget about it, okay?"

"Okay," Catherine replied softly, blushing a little.

"Good then. So, do you wanna show us again now?"

"Like – just sitting down like this?" she asked, peering from Brad to me as she lifted the front of her skirt. We both looked down at her crotch, and she leaned back and pulled her skirt up over her hips. She was watching my face, and I glanced up to meet her eyes.

Brad reached for one of her tits and felt it gently. Her gaze lowered to his hand. "Your nipples are responsive, aren't they?" he said to her.

"They're very sensitive tonight. Especially without my bra on."

"Yeah? Do you wanna take your top off too after this guy's gone – let us look at your tits while we're chatting and waiting for Tom?"

"They're not much to look at, though," Catherine uttered.

"I wanna look!" I smiled, and she glanced up and blushed a little at that.

"Me too!" Brad added. "But about Reg – maybe if you came and sat on the other side here and tucked your legs up. That way he'd be able to see your pussy from behind, but it'd be kinda subtle."

"Over there?" Catherine asked, standing and stepping around Brad's legs, keeping hold of her skirt. Brad was setting a cushion for her and I leant in behind and felt up between her thighs. "Hey, you!" she complained, pushing against my head, but only gently, and I managed to work my middle finger up her again.

Brad grinned. "Is she still wet?"

"Yeah. Not like before but wet enough."

Catherine clutched a handful of my hair, and she crouched just slightly, curling her hips back and opening herself to me a little more. I withdrew my finger then forced it up her again, and her nails dug into my scalp.

I smiled. "She's juicing up now."

"Come on, don't be greedy!" Brad complained.

Catherine was more open than earlier, and I could feel her juices swirling around my finger. "Are you gonna let this old guy have a look?"

"Uh huh."

"Do you wanna go get ready now?" I said to her, carefully removing my finger and smearing the thick fluid around the lips of her pussy.

"Okay," she said softly, and she stepped across to stand before Brad.

"Just sort of lean over against the arm and tuck your feet up. We'll see how that looks," he said to her.

Catherine still had her skirt bunched around her waist. She sat and lifted her feet up onto the sofa.

"Yeah, that's good," Brad went on, and he gently rolled her and felt up behind her legs, slicing two fingers in between the lips of her pussy then forcing them inside of her.

"Uhh…huhh." Catherine moaned, gripping the arm of the sofa, and Brad got up onto his knees and started fucking her with his hand. His arm was jolting back and forth, his two fingers thrusting in and out and his thumb massaging her clit again. Her eyes were shut tight, and her body seemed to flex with her hips arching up off the sofa as she began to shudder. Brad stopped. He had his fingers fully embedded in her, and he held firm while her body pulsed.

Catherine's eyes opened to stare blankly for a moment before they focused. She looked back at us two men. "You're going to wear me out if you keep doing that."

"Are you complaining?" Brad asked, sucking his fingers whilst holding her gaze.

"Um – no!" she replied, still grinning, and she straightened her skirt down a bit as she sat up. "But I wish I had my wine."

"I'll go see what's happening with it," Brad declared, and he left again.

Catherine

"It was nicer that time."

Foley nodded. "You seemed more open somehow."

"I know. I was a bit nervous the first time."

"Are you okay now? You're not getting sore or anything?"

"No, I'm fine. I'm still tingling down there, but it feels nice. And anyway I don't mind if I end up a bit sore tomorrow."

"And when he used two fingers, was that okay?"

"Yeah, but I liked what you did too. And next time you do it to me you can use two fingers if you want to. I won't mind."

"So, does that mean it's okay to do it again later?"

I giggled. "I don't know. I'm just saying it felt nice."

"Well, what about Tom? I wonder what's happened to him."

"I don't know. I might call him. Can I have my bag, please?"

Foley gave me my bag and left me to use the bathroom. I gave my wayward boyfriend a call but got rid of him quickly because Brad came back, his eyes all over me immediately he closed the door. I just pushed back my hair and smiled at him. I was kneeling on the couch. He approached and circled me. I sat with my legs tucked up to one side.

"Did you get Tom?" Foley asked, returning from the bathroom.

"Yes, he's downstairs with some friends of ours. I told him we were just having a few drinks, so he said he'd come up later."

"And what about old Reg with the wine?"

"Yeah, he's on his way up. They forgot all about it," Brad explained. "And you're good with him coming in, aren't you?" he asked me, leaning back to look up behind my legs.

"I'm still a little bit nervous about it, but yes."

"That's good, and do you just wanna move your legs a little bit? Maybe move this top one forward so you open up a bit more for him?" He guided me so that my lower leg straightened and the top one was bent up, which had the effect of opening my wet, reddened pussy behind my legs. He touched it gently, working his fingertips into my juices and smearing them, then he forced two long, thick digits up me.

"Uhh..hh.." I moaned but bit down on my lip and just braced against the strong hand behind me.

I held Foley's gaze steadily while the other man fingered me again. I rested my head upon the arm of the sofa, and allowed him to rock my body with each thrust into me. I just stared at my friend and let this other man enjoy the feel of my pussy. It wasn't so much that it felt nice for me – more so that he was enjoying it and getting off doing it to me.

"Are you okay?" Foley asked me softly.

"Uh huh. I don't mind," I uttered in reply, sort of lifting my bottom and grinding a little as Brad felt deep inside of me. I looked back over my shoulder and watched his face. He tilted for a closer look and used his thumb to peel my cunt open. I flared my hips and waited while he had a look inside of me.

"Ooh that's fucking nice," he groaned.

Foley got up and leant in behind me for a closer look too. I was mesmerized now and tingling all over with the excitement of being so lewdly on display. I flared my hips further to make it easier for them to see. "Mmm you can use both thumbs and stretch me if you want."

The man, Brad, inserted his other thumb, and I took a breath and bit down hard on my lip as he stretched my cunt open wider.

"Fuck yeah," Foley groaned too, and he reached through and parted my hood to reveal my swollen clit. He held my delicate folds apart with his fingers and rubbed me there with his other hand.

"That's it, man, make her cum with her cunt open like this," Brad said, and my belly immediately clenched, and my orgasm from before resurged and pulsed through me.

"Fuck yeah, look at her tunnel trying to suck," Foley said, examining me intently.

The other man inserted two thick digits again and resumed finger-banging me. The intensity of my orgasm immediately increased and I just gripped the arm of the couch and kept my hips flared so he could enjoy the feel of me throbbing on his fingers. Letting him imagine it was his cock that my pussy was trying to suck on like that. His cock with his huge balls all full of sperm and ready to burst and flood me.

"Uhhh..hhh…hhh," I moaned as my belly clenched hard again, and I squirmed my legs together and had to twist away from being penetrated now.

Foley

There was a knock at the door, and Brad withdrew his fingers from Catherine's cunt and wiped them on her inner thigh. He got up and moved to the chair beside where I sat back down then called for the guy to come in.

"Hello, Reg. How are you?"

"Fine thanks, and you, Brad?"

"Great! We're just having a little party up here. Thanks for doing the run for us."

"No, you're welcome. I'm sorry we forgot, but I've had so many checking in tonight."

"Foley and Catherine, this is Reg, a good friend of mine since I've been virtually living here."

We nodded greetings, and Reg's eyes flashed down to Catherine's legs briefly. "Looks like a fun party," he suggested to Brad.

"Just a few friends getting together, if you know what I mean." Brad grinned. "Stay for a beer?"

"No, I'd better get back to it," Reg motioned with the bottle of wine.

127

"Yeah, just pop it on the coffee table thanks, buddy."

The coffee table was beside the sofa, and the old guy leant directly behind Catherine. She'd straightened up a bit, but her pussy was still blatantly exposed, and the doorman's gaze fixed upon it as he placed the ice bucket down. Brad was smiling over. He winked but Catherine just glared back at him.

Old Reg was opening the bottle, his gaze remained fixed upon Catherine's wet and obviously used pussy. She smoothed her skirt, edging it down a bit. Reg looked away, sort of nervously. "Should I pour?" he asked, checking with Brad.

"No, we'll get that. But how are things? How's your wife?"

"Mad at me." Reg grinned, his eyes roaming and pausing before lifting again, and he replaced the bottle in the bucket and casually stepped around to lean on the back of the sofa. He was out of Catherine's line of sight there, and his eyes lowered, fixing directly on her cunt.

"It's okay, she likes us checking her out," Brad said, and Catherine turned and peered back up at Reg's face while her fingers twisted the hem of her skirt. It was as if she would pull it down but she didn't.

Reg smiled, shaking his head. "Oh, to be young again," he said with a sigh, and after meeting Catherine's eyes for a moment, he looked back down at her pussy. He leant a little and tilted his head to examine it. Catherine's blush surged as she watched him. She also edged her upper leg forward and opened herself more for him. "Ooh that's nice," Reg groaned. "That's a very pretty pussy, love."

"Uh huh," Catherine uttered. "I'm glad you all think so."

"Stick your fingers in, Reg. She won't mind," Brad said evenly.

The old guy gulped and looked from Brad to me then back at Catherine's cunt. He gulped hard again, Catherine just glaring back up at him and blushing wildly.

Brad chuckled. "Go on, man, you know you want to."

Catherine shot him a look but glared back up at the old guy. He gulped hard again and flashed a glance at Brad and I again.

"Go on, quick, before she changes her mind," Brad encouraged.

The old room service waiter reached down and rubbed into Catherine's wet opening. "Uhh..hhh…" she moaned and sort of whimpered as he inserted a finger into her.

He inserted all the way then pulled it almost all the way out, then inserted again and seemed to feel around inside of her. "Oooh that's nice."

Catherine looked away, her head turning and her eyes averting forward to stare at the arm of the couch as she flared her hips and presented herself for the old guy. He worked his finger in and out of her, tilting in close to examine her cunt, like Brad and I had a moment ago. I met her blank gaze. She was blushing deeply, her eyes coming to light and rolling away embarrassingly.

The old guy smacked her bottom and stood. "Whew!" He left Catherine pulling her skirt down to cover herself and walked from behind the sofa. "Well, I'll let you kids get back to it."

Brad chuckled. "Thanks, Reg. See you tomorrow?"

"No, I'm off this weekend. See you Monday."

*

As soon as the door closed a cushion hit Brad in the face. "I can't believe you let him do that to me!" Catherine declared, her face still bright red but a smile breaking through. Then she jumped up and climbed on top of Brad, her hands clawing playfully at his throat while he laughed and pretended to fight her off. He only held her away a little, though, then his hands went up her top, and he lifted it and sucked on one of her tits. "No! I want my wine now," she demanded, pushing and breaking away from him, and she came over to where I was pouring it for her. "I can't believe I just did that," she said, panting and smiling. "Gosh, I hope I never see him in the street."

"It was fun, though, wasn't it?" Brad asked her.

I sat on the couch and Catherine stepped across beside me. "It is now, but I was terrified a minute ago." She giggled, sitting back against the far end and pushing me with her toes. "And you're just as bad!" she scolded, but she allowed me to lift her feet onto my lap, and I began massaging them while we chatted.

"So, did I hear correctly that you guys are related?" Brad ventured at one point.

"No, we're just friends, but it kinda feels like we are," I explained.

"Too bad. I think it would be hot! I've got a few cousins I wish were, well, friendly!" Brad grinned, and Catherine blushed a little. "Your boyfriend's done well too," he went on. "I mean, when I was married I often fantasized about other guys with my wife, but I never said anything, and I dunno, maybe things would've turned out better."

"Well, we kind of met at a group thing," Catherine started in response. "Plus, we both like stories."

"What kind of stories?" Brad leant in with interest.

"They're usually about couples where another man would have sex with the girl."

"Yeah, but give us some details! You know, for example?"

"No! I'm not telling you!" Catherine complained.

"Come on. Just a few little details," Brad pleaded. "What's your fav?"

"I don't know. Maybe the ones where the woman would be sort of forced to do it."

Brad grinned. "Forced?"

"Well, not really forced. Just where she'd have to let other men have sex with her to pay off a debt or something. Or if there was someone with a hold over them, like a boss or whatever, and she'd have to let the guy have sex with her to keep her husband's job."

"And there's always just one other guy?"

"Not always. Some of the stories are about more than one. Like with the husband being just a worker and she'd have to let all the supervisors and managers have her."

Brad slipped from his chair and crawled across. Catherine was lying on her back, but he lifted from beneath her leg and rolled her onto her side. I slipped further along the sofa out of the way so the guy was free to manipulate her. Then Brad pulled her skirt up and forced his hand between her legs, rubbing into her pussy for a minute then inserting his fingers into her. She held to the arm of the sofa and arched her hips, and he started pumping them slowly in and out.

I watched her face. Her eyes were closed, but when they opened she turned her head to the side and peered back at me. Again there was nothing in her expression to suggest she was enjoying it, but she was arching up to meet the thrusts of Brad's hand.

Her eyes closed again and suddenly Brad held firm, and I saw the slight tremors pulse through my friend's body. Brad withdrew his fingers and mashed them into her folds, rubbing her juices into the lips of her pussy, then he started feeling her anus. He worked around it, massaging the tip of his middle finger in before he slowly inserted it, forcing it all the way and turning his hand then withdrawing it again. Catherine's eyes opened, and I met them once more. They slowly closed as Brad pushed forward, and she bit down on her lip, but again her body arched to meet him.

"Might duck down and see if the kitchen's still open," Brad said casually. "Sometimes there's left over pizza if you get them when they're closing up." He withdrew his finger and smoothed Catherine's skirt back down, then he stood. "You guy's hungry?" he asked, and we both nodded. "Okay – won't be long," he added, adjusting his erection, and left.

*

Catherine turned back over and sat fixing her top, which had ridden up her back. She held my gaze as I edged a little closer, and I reached in under her legs and felt inside the lips of her pussy. She was hot and open, and I pushed two fingers in a little then massaged her juices into her labia and outer lips. "Do you want me to lie over your lap again?" she asked softly, and I nodded.

She lay back placing her head down on the arm of the sofa and put her feet on my lap. She arched her hips as I pushed two fingers up her. I forced them as far as I could and held firmly while rocking against her with my arm. "I like it when you finger me," Catherine uttered sweetly, and I pumped her a few times hard then held firmly again. I withdrew and felt her other little hole. I used a third finger, and as I slid a finger back into her pussy and pressed my thumb on her clit, I inserted the middle finger into her anus.

Catherine writhed against my hand, rolling her hips and grinding on my fingers, so I started thrusting into her again. "Mmm that's nice like that," she whimpered, arching up higher and gripping the arm of the sofa, and I kept pumping her with long, steady movements until suddenly her inner walls clamped down on my fingers, and I held firmly up her while her entire body throbbed around them. "Can you feel that?" she asked, peering back at me, and her eyes closed, and she continued to throb. "Mmm," she breathed heavily, reaching back and pushing against my arm.

I pulled my fingers out and she rolled to her side. I shuffled back away from her, and she rolled over onto her back, her hand going to the hem of her skirt and stretching it down to cover her crotch. Her other arm was bent up over her face, and she just lay there like that measuring her breaths.

I collected her wine glass and refilled it then went back to her side. She sat up and took the glass, glancing at the bulge in my pants, offering a little smile as a thank you. Then I moved back to my chair and let her get herself together before speaking.

"Are you okay?" I asked warmly.

"Yeah, I'm fine. I just had a little head spin that time, but I think it was because of the way I was lying. Too much blood rushing to my head."

"Well, pizza's actually a good idea. I hope he gets some," I suggested.

"Me too. I'm starving," Catherine agreed. "And I've got absolutely no energy left."

I smiled. "Do you want some of mine?"

"Some of yours?" she asked, a little hesitantly.

I wasn't serious, but having gone that far I decided to go on. "I really need get a load off in you?"

"Um now?" Catherine asked softly.

"I've been hard for hours. It'll only take a minute – literally!"

My friend blushed a little, glancing away, then her eyes lifted tentatively. "Is it okay if I just let you? I mean, I don't think I've got the energy to do much."

"That's fine. Seriously, as soon as I get in there I'm just going to start cumming, and by the feel of this I'm going to absolutely flood you."

"Okay then," Catherine uttered, peering up at me as I stood. "Should I lie back down?"

"No, come around here," I said, stepping behind the sofa, and she stood and followed me. "Bend over for me," I instructed, and she leaned over and rested on the back of the sofa.

I lifted Catherine's skirt up over her back and freed my aching erection. Then I probed her with the head until it went in, and I forced it all the way up her. "Aaah fuck!" I grunted immediately, and I pumped her a few times and drove up under her and held. "Yeah, that's close," I breathed, then I pumped her a few more times and held again with the tingling sensation rising in my loins. I pumped again and the sensation surged up my shaft and erupted with a massive burst.

"Oh fuck! Can you feel that?" I gasped. My cock was gushing the pent up load of cum that had been aching my balls. Catherine moaned a soft response, her hand touching my hip and holding me close. I collapsed over her back, still fully imbedded in her and still throbbing. "Thank you," I breathed into her hair.

"Just hold it in me until you finish. I can still feel it," she whispered, arching her head back next to me and still holding me close.

"I'm going soft," I said.

"But don't pull out yet. Just move it around inside of me. I feel so wet now."

"Do you wanna cum again?" I asked softly, pulling back. I could feel my cock fold, but it easily popped back up into her.

Catherine giggled. "No, I don't, silly! I'm not this wet from me, it's from you. And I can feel *that* too, but don't think you're going to do it again just yet."

My cock had flexed inside of her. It was rousing, so I pressed up behind her and started gently rolling my pelvis. I was soon fully erect again. "Been wanting to do this again for ages too." I said, withdrawing then slowly pushing back into her.

Catherine had her head resting upon her folded arms. She was watching over her shoulder. "I can't believe I let you without a condom. I haven't even let Tom lately."

"So, you always make him use rubbers?"

"Yes. I can't go on the pill at the moment, so it's the easiest way."

"So, this was definitely a bit risky, eh?" I went on, forcing myself up against her. "A chance of you getting preggers. That's so hot," I teased.

"Hmm – only a small chance."

"Yeah, well, I like trying to get you pregnant, Catherine," I whispered into her hair, and she arched back up beneath me, so I humped her a few times quickly.

"Do you want to cum in me again?" she breathed, meeting my mouth.

"Yeah I do, but I want you to let this other guy fuck you next. You will, won't you?"

"Mmm I guess," Catherine moaned, and I could feel her fingers rubbing the underside of my cock as she worked her clit. I started fucking her firmly but slowly, and suddenly her pussy contracted around my shaft, so I held still – but she was incredibly tight and I couldn't help myself. I thrust a few more times and erupted once again, and her warm little fingers closed over my balls and held them softly as I pulsed inside of her.

Catherine peered back, smiling lightly through her blush.

I grinned. "Oops!"

"It felt like even more than the first time," she said softly.

"I dunno. I don't think it was, but it was another pretty big load." I was numb and spent, and my cock slipped from her.

"Hmm, and are you satisfied now?" she went on sweetly.

"Yeah. For a while. But after Brad, I might have another turn."

"And I *might* let you," she teased, pushing me away and standing to fix her clothing back into place.

I walked around the sofa and collapsed onto it. Catherine went to her bag and folded some tissues then dabbed them up between her legs while I watched quietly.

She glanced over at me and smiled. "What?" she complained.

"Nothing, just watching."

"Well, it was starting to dribble down my legs," she defended and tossed the tissues at me.

"So, just let it run down your legs. That's hot."

She rolled eyes, smiling through her blush. "Hmm, I guess."

"My huge load up you and dripping out." I tilted to look at her cunt from behind. "Yeah, just let it."

"Uh huh, I will if any more drips out. If you insist."

"Yeah, I insist," I said evenly, squeezing my resurgent cock. "I'm definitely gonna fuck you again after this other guy too. Add another load after he pumps his into you. Make sure you drip good and proper all night."

"Um okay," my friend agreed softly. "If you need to you always can with me, Foley. You know that."

"Yeah. I know," I said and tugged her hand, guiding her to sit beside me. I smoothed her hair and kissed her softly. "You're a little cum doll, aren't you, Cath." I kissed her again. "Any man who wants could get a load off in you if he tried hard enough, eh!"

"Mmm, but I don't like it when a man's balls are all full and uncomfortable," she breathed into my mouth, making my cock flex hard again. "I'd rather just let him empty them in me," she went on breathily. "In my mouth or in my cunt..."

"Aw fuck."

*

Brad returned with a tray of pizza slices, and we ate hungrily while chatting. Apparently Tom had joined an after-work party with the staff and was settled in. After we'd eaten, Brad went to the fridge for more beers, and I caught Catherine's hand as she was stepping past and pulled her onto the sofa again. She pushed at me but not seriously, and I forced her onto her back and felt up under her skirt.

"Wait! Just let me have a sip of my wine first," she said softly.

I handed her the glass and waited while she drank some. Then she gave it back to me and lay down, lifting her skirt up over her belly. "Just gently at first," she said, glancing up at Brad as he approached the back of the sofa.

"Do you want some oil?" Brad asked.

"What sort is it?"

"Just baby oil."

Catherine blushed a little and nodded, and Brad left and returned with a small bottle, which he handed to me. He also had a towel. "Just slip this underneath so we don't make a mess of the sofa."

Catherine lifted her bottom while the towel was spread beneath her. I poured oil onto my fingers and felt into her, slipping in easily. I forced two of them up her and held while she rolled down against my fist, fucking herself on them. "Do you want to do the other as well?" she asked with a blush. "Just with one again."

I smiled and withdrew enough to position a third finger. I inserted it into her little hole and resumed working her, but I mostly allowed her to set the pace. After a few minutes I started thrusting into her a little. Her eyes were closed, her breathing ragged. She arched herself up off the towel and braced, and I pumped her hard and fast until she bucked, then I forced my fingers deep and held firm while the walls of her pussy contracted and throbbed.

Both of us men watched her body pulse through her orgasm, and when she collapsed, I worked her juices into her hot sloppy folds and opened her a little to see how red she was deep inside. I held her pussy lips apart, and Brad leaned down to have a look too. He also slipped a finger into her and pulled her cunt open a little wider.

Catherine was watching us. She was blushing and biting down on her lip. Brad started rubbing her, and I sat back a bit. He lifted her leg and made her roll over. I moved out of his way and took a seat across the room. Catherine rested her head on the arm of the couch. Her eyes were on me as Brad poured more baby oil then rubbed it around a little and forced a finger up her anus. Her eyes widened and she bit down on the arm of the leather couch.

"Are you still okay?" I asked her.

She nodded. "It hurts a little bit but I don't mind."

Brad had his middle finger all the way in and was feeling around. Catherine looked back at him, and he smiled. Her blush deepened, and he started thrusting his finger in and out. "Does your boyfriend ever play with your arse? You feel tight."

"He doesn't do anything like that," she uttered, but her eyes closed, and she squirmed back against Brad's hand as he inserted a finger into her pussy and pressed his thumb on her clit as well. He vibrated his fingers inside her, and within a minute she was convulsing in orgasm yet again.

Brad rubbed her sloppy, reddened gash until she settled, then he knelt in behind her and freed his cock. It was solid. "Do you want me to use a condom?" he asked her.

"You don't have to," Catherine uttered shyly, peering back over her shoulder.

"You sure?"

"Uh huh. It's exciting – the chance of getting pregnant to you." She looked to me as well. "I was actually late with my period after that time we went rafting."

She laid her head down and held my eyes. Brad opened her pussy lips with the head of his cock, and her eyes widened as he rocked forward and filled her with the length of his shaft. "So, you've risked it with other men before, eh?"

"Uh huh. I've been on the pill lately but my doctor took me off it for a while."

Catherine maintained eye contact with me as she was slowly and rhythmically jolted, and when Brad grunted and held firm her eyes intensified a little. Then they closed softly, and she waited while the guy finished himself off, slowly fucking her and playing in her with his cock and feeling in her anus with his thumb. "There you go, baby. There's a nice healthy load for you."

He pulled out, and Catherine edged around and tugged her skirt down. She bit her lip, peering at the guy. "So, you don't mind that you don't even know me and you just came in me unprotected?"

Brad grinned. "I wouldn't mind fathering another child. An attractive girl like you – I'd be all for it."

147

"I agree," I declared forthrightly. "You'd look beautiful pregnant, Catherine."

Catherine smiled shyly. "Well, it depends if I'm still ovulating. I might've just finished – not sure."

"So, when is your next period due?" Brad asked, stroking hair from my friend's face.

She blushed. "About a week or so."

Brad nodded. "You'll have to give me a call, let me know."

"Okay – I will. And I'm still not going to let Tom, so it will be to one of you men if I do fall pregnant."

*

I poured more wine, and we sat around chatting and laughing. Catherine had her legs tucked up, and from behind them we guys could see her puffy little slit quite nicely. After a while the smooth opening between her pussy lips began to fill with milky fluid, though, and Brad had stopped talking and was leaning over staring at it. He touched her thigh and peeled her open a bit, and a jelly-like glob of semen oozed out.

He chuckled. "Yeah, definitely proud of that effort."

I stood and approached his shoulder, and Catherine peered up at me. "There's a small vibrator in my purse if you men want to use something else in me."

I opened her purse and found a five inch gold thing that was quite slim. I turned it on and smeared it through the fluid oozing from her then inserted it into her anus. I started sliding it in and out, and Catherine rolled over a little more to give me access. Brad slipped two fingers up her pussy, and she moaned softly and laid her head down on the arm of the sofa. Brad started finger fucking her hard and fast, and I worked the vibe in and out of her arse until she convulsed in yet another orgasm.

Brad freed his erection and plowed into her from behind, humping wildly, and making loud squelching noises, until he was jammed right up her, grinding into her and ejaculating.

Catherine

"Mmm that feels so nice," I uttered teasingly, peering back over my shoulder and biting down on my lip and smile. I could feel the strong jets of cum gushing into me, and as the man on my back started moving again, I could feel how wet I was from him.

I love being all gooey and slick from a man's semen. I had really missed that the past month since Tom had agreed to be careful.

I peered back over my shoulder at both men. "Promise you won't tease my boyfriend too much about cumming inside me like this, okay?"

They both chuckled. Foley was feeling his cock again too, so it looked like he was going to need to fuck me again. They looked to each other to work out whose turn it was. I wouldn't have minded if the old room service man came back and joined in with them. I was a bit numb from all the fingering and too many orgasms to count.

I love being used like this though. I just love men getting excited for sex and taking me for their pleasure.

*

That night in the hotel room, Brad, the complete stranger to me, and my friend Foley both fucked me three times, cumming inside my pussy each time. They did end up teasing my boyfriend mercilessly when he finally came back from the party downstairs.

That was my last week with Tom though, before he declared himself to be gay rather than bisexual. He left me for a new boyfriend, which was fine, and I got my period right on time too, so all was good.

Foley was back and forth then disappeared completely, away with his sales job, and I heard he met someone and settled down. I also met a nice man by the name of Ashton though. We dated for a while and got married. Which was the end of my wild fun times with multiple men partners.

It was the end for a while at least...

** Oh yeah, for a while! **

Nude Beach Surprise

Catherine

I wasn't sure if everything was supposed to change or not, now that I was married. The thing was that my husband Ashton knew me. He knew my history and what I was like, and he obviously liked me... and presumably the way I was, which was something he had taken advantage of.

Well, enjoyed might be a better word for it.

I think all men take advantage of me, and I love that they do.

This has been happening since I was barely of age and this married guy rescued me drunk from a party and took me to his bed for the night, where he fucked me several times then went to sleep and left me to make my own way home.

That was my first time with sexual intercourse. I'd given a boy a blowjob at the party earlier, and I also gave one to the older man who ultimately saw me home safe.

I learnt that day that I love giving blowjobs and being taken to bed by guys my own age, married ones, and old men too.

My next little adventure was on holidays at a beach resort with my parents, where I was talked into going topless at first, then fully nude at a secluded part of the beach. That was by another married guy and he shared me with the older maintenance man from the resort. Plus there was the guy from next door who was there with his parents too, and I let him play with me a bit after the older men had.

Then my next adventure after that was on this remote island where there were dirty old fishermen and these three young guys. That was lots of fun flashing the old fishermen. I love the way guys look at me, and it was so exciting teasing the old men on their boats by walking along the pier above them in short skirts.

Yes that turned out to be a really fun holiday, where I got to have lots of sex with the three boys my age, and I was lucky enough to have a chance to suck this lonely old fisherman's cock for him.

Mmm that was so yucky and yummy at the same time!

And my next adventure after that was on a weekend rafting trip where I shared a tent with three very horny guys, one of whom is a friend of my now husband Ashton.

So yes, Ashton knows all about me, and now that we were married, I didn't know quite what to expect. Especially since there was this one night just before the wedding when his uncle fucked me... and Ashton knows that he did!

A couple of months into our marriage, we hadn't really talked. Ashton had organized a week away, and I was determined to bring it up and ask what he wanted me to do... whether I should behave more conservatively now. I thought it would be perfectly reasonable if my husband wanted me all to himself.

Of course it would, right?

Ashton

"Oh my gosh, where are we?"

My beautiful wife Catherine had stirred. She was yawning and peering around at the dozen or so campervans and scattering of tents. I had hired a fully equipped RV for a week and had managed to keep our destination a surprise.

"This is it, sweetheart – the beach, the sun, good camp food, plenty of beer and wine, and a week of wild sex."

"Huh. You hope! Although it does look nice. And smell those barbeques. Gosh I'm hungry!"

We cooked indoors and ate dinner before setting up the annex. It was just on nightfall, and by the time we were organized and ready to relax with a drink, the camp grounds had settled to crackling fires and small groups of people sitting around chatting and laughing.

"There aren't any children," Catherine announced suddenly.

"Err – no. Strange that, isn't it?"

The campervan next door had been in silence, but an older couple came along and greeted us. They were carrying bags and towels and had obviously spent the day at the beach. They introduced themselves as Roger and Liz. Roger would have been in his late 50s, maybe a little older, and his wife looked about mid-40s. They were British.

"Don't be daft, love – can't you see they're romancing in the moonlight there." Liz had suggested they pack their things away and join us for a drink. Her husband was hustling her along.

Catherine giggled. "No, that'd be nice. He doesn't know how to romance me and they're all having parties."

Roger smiled. "Right you are then. We'll toss this lot and be back directly."

"They seem nice," I suggested when they'd gone.

"They do. I hope they're staying. It will be good to have friendly neighbours."

I moved over behind Catherine and bent to kiss her neck. "So, do you like it? Did I do good?"

"Yes, you did good. We must be so close to the water – it'll be nice listening to it in bed."

"What, you mean almost a romantic setting?"

"Well, possibly!" Catherine kissed me softly. "I didn't mean that about you not being romantic."

"Oh no, that's fine. I'd have picked a different spot if I was thinking of romance. This is more about having fun and being free and relaxed."

Roger and Liz returned with chairs and a few bottles of wine. The four of us sat up until the early hours talking and getting drunk. It would have been mid-morning when I woke to Catherine shaking me and peering out the window.

"My gosh, that man's naked!" she cried.

"What? Where? What man?"

"There! Oh no, there's another one!"

I crawled up to the window. There were two men standing there chatting away without a stitch of clothing on. "Well, they're just being free and relaxed," I tried casually.

"What – this is a nude beach?"

157

"It's optional. Not everyone's naked. Look, there's some people with clothes on." I was trying not to laugh.

Catherine was taking it in. "You scumbag! Married five minutes and you brought me to a nude beach!" She had another look out the window, and when she turned back there was the hint of a smile. "There's no way I'm doing that."

There was a loud knock at the door. "Anyone for a cuppa?"

Catherine and I looked at each other. "You make sure he's got clothes on!" Catherine warned with a giggle.

"Morning, Roger, come in if you're decent," I called out.

Roger laughed. "Decent as I get." He struggled through the door carrying a tray with a teapot and cups and saucers. His swimmers were brief and sported a sizable bulge in front. It's all he had on.

Catherine was in a t-shirt and panties, and the older man quickly looked her over as she tied a skirt around her waist.

Liz brought eggs, bacon and sausages, and we ate and laughed at Catherine's dilemma. She stood her ground though, and when we moved camp to the beach, she had on one of her more modest bikinis.

"Do you mind if we indulge?" Roger asked her. He had left his wife swimming and stood before us getting ready to lie down on his towel with his thumbs just sticking through the top of his swimmers.

Catherine giggled. "Feel free. Just about everyone else is."

"You really should try it," Roger declared, smiling as he peeled his swimmers down. His cock sprung free, obviously suffering the effects of the cold water. It was thick though, and his balls were huge.

"Oh my gosh!" Catherine was blushing and trying to look away.

"No, not to worry. It gets bigger. Some fresh air and sunshine, you'll be impressed soon enough."

"No. I mean, oh my gosh, another naked man!"

"I see. Well, how about you, Ashton old son, care to indulge?"

I stood up and stripped my shorts. Catherine squealed in delight and covered her face with her hands. I dropped to my knees behind her and started rubbing sunscreen into her back and shoulders. "You'd better put some on that," she warned, giggling and pointing at my dick.

"I thought you might do that for me."

"No chance! I'm going to read my book and leave you natives to do what you want."

Catherine

It was interesting watching the nude men wandering around. I'd been to that one nude beach before, but that seemed to be all about the men I was with wanting to get a look at me. I was enjoying it the other way around, especially because most of the men walking by and smiling at me were mature and with huge balls.

I love cocks, and I love balls too. They're so fascinating and nice to hold and kiss while they're filling with cum.

A surge of tingles rushed through me and lit up my sex as I watched this huge fat man approach and thought of his balls filling with cum. His were shaved bald and really droopy in their sac. His penis was short and stubby, his balls hanging a long way below the bulbous head of it. The eyelet was huge too, and I had to swallow at my watering mouth as I imagined sucking him and being rewarded with pulses of thick gooey semen shooting from it.

Mmm oh my gosh, Catherine, stop it!

I took a big breath and looked away from the man standing there only a few paces away. Roger was lying there on his back with his nice long penis sunning itself across his groin. I lay there with my head on my folded arms just looking at it until his wife sat up and caught me before I blushed and averted my gaze.

The problem was that there was actually nowhere to look. There were six men right then standing or lying facing us, and they all had their cocks and yummy balls on display. What was a girl supposed to look at?

I turned over and sat facing away from them for a while, joining Liz in looking at our husbands' cocks. I felt entitled to enjoy her husband's now, since she was making no attempt to disguise her interest in Ashton's.

We ended up spending a few hours there sunbathing and swimming, but I refused to take off my bikini at all, not even my top. I would have been happy to, but I knew what would happen if I did. I was by far the youngest and slimmest woman on the beach, and if I had undressed, all the dirty old men would have gathered around and ignored the other women, which would have been unfair to them and embarrassing for me.

No, I was happy being the voyeur today and teasing all the old men by denying them. The whole thing turned me on though, and I couldn't get my pants off quick enough once back in the privacy of the RV with my nudie husband.

"Aw fuck that's wet, baby," he groaned as I squished down on him.

I still had on my bikini top. I was straddling him on the bed, pinning him down by the wrists like I was in control for a change. I love cowgirl and ground myself through a nice orgasm before Aston flipped me over and fucked me for his own pleasure.

"Uh huh take me, Ashton. I can't stop thinking about all those old men's balls I saw today!"

Ashton

"Will you wear something sexy tonight?" I asked my wife. We were to visit Roger and Liz for drinks. "Roger's wife's been naked all day, and he hasn't seen you at all yet."

"I know, but now that we're married it seems kind of wrong to be taking my bikini off in public like that. Certainly not my bottoms!"

"Sure, sweetheart, but you'd like him to have a bit of a look, wouldn't you? I know he wants to."

"Does he? Did he say that?"

"Sure he said it. How many times today did he ask if you were *ready to indulge yet*? He's dying to get a look at you."

I was getting dressed. Catherine sat up in bed and reached for my hand, pulling me closer and getting me to sit on the bed beside her. "So, is this just about showing me to him?" she asked softly. "Is that all you want to happen?"

I shrugged. "I dunno. Maybe – maybe not?"

Catherine fiddled with the edge of the sheet for a moment before looking up. "I was wondering if you were going to want to do anything because of what happened with your uncle. You haven't talked about it at all since the wedding."

I was fiddling with the edge of the sheet as well. "I know, but I still think about it all the time... It's hard to get the picture out of my mind. And the thought of it!"

"The thought of it?" Catherine questioned softly.

"Yeah, the idea that he's been with you. It's sort of weird, but sometimes when I look at you I kinda think of it as you being marked by him. Like he's had his dick in you and nothing's gonna change that."

Catherine was blushing. "You think of that when you look at me?"

"Well no! Only once in a while. Like when I'm watching you undress or in the bath or something," I added quickly. "And it's a good thought overall. It's not like I regret what happened that much or anything. Like I said, it's kind of exciting to think about it."

I kissed my wife and smoothed her hair. I was boning up over the pictures in my head.

"Yes, but we're married now," she uttered. "Unless you want to look at me and think of another man having marked me as well."

"Do you ever think about it like that?" I was suddenly anxious as well as excited. "Do you ever think of it as if my uncle got to touch you somewhere very special… that he got to touch you there with his dick and it felt so good for him he left a little deposit as his marker?"

Catherine giggled at that. "Actually, he left quite a large deposit, and every time he looks at me he reminds me about it." She held my gaze, blushing as she went on. "He always looks at my legs, trying to see up my skirt or dress, and sometimes I let him, since he's already had sex with me."

"Aw fuck yeah, that's good, baby. You should let Uncle get a look sometimes, since he's fucked you. And are you gonna let this guy Roger have sex with you as well?" I asked hopefully.

Catherine took a moment to respond. "It's exciting to think about being taken by another man now that I'm seriously not supposed to," she said softly. "It would be exciting with you watching. Especially if he's allowed to have me without protection and cum inside me."

I kissed her lips. "It's not like the thought of sharing you with other men is anything too outlandish, baby. You know Foley used to tell me all about your adventures before we got together."

"I know. But I still don't want to know the details of what you dirty men talk about, thank you very much!"

I chuckled. "Agreed. So, let's start making some new details of our own?"

Catherine moaned into another kiss. "Mmm okay... but what should I wear to show off for this man? I didn't bring anything sexy because you said we'd be camping."

"What about those shorts you wore to the beach today? I could see your bikini pants when you were sitting down. How about wearing those without panties?" I was kissing my wife's neck and nibbling her ear. "And what about that stretchy top I like – the one that's always falling off your shoulder?"

"The crocheted one?" Catherine asked excitedly.

"Yeah, this one." I plucked it from the drawer.

Catherine

I took the top my husband had picked out and smiled through a blush. "Actually, for one detail, it was an extremely large deposit your uncle left in me that time. I was a bit drunk but I remember it clearly, and he was drunk too, but that just meant it took him a long time to cum... He was actually in me for half an hour before he finally came... He stayed hard the whole time though, just screwing me really slow and deep and teasing me about it being the last chance before we got married. And when he eventually came I was really exhausted, and the only thing I could feel was his dick squirting and squirting!"

I looked down at where my husband was squeezing his cock to one side in his pants. , then I peered back up at the blank look on his face.

I knew for sure right then that he wanted me to be fucked by other men.... that I was going to be a shared wife.

The idea of being easy for men and pleasing them sexually has always thrilled me. It was good that I was going to be able to be my natural self with Ashton. He was obviously excited about being cuckolded, like with his uncle, and it seemed he was still interested in experiencing that as my actual husband.

I was so excited with this, but I wanted to make it even better for my man, so I decided to play coy and make him feel like he was talking me into flashing or stripping for these older men.

Hmm, this is going to be so fun!

Ashton

I had to virtually drag Catherine out the door when she was dressed. Her top was loose at the bottom and didn't cover her bellybutton. The neckline was broad and easily slipped from a shoulder, and the fabric was loosely woven, so without a bra her dark little nipples were prominent. She looked so cute in shorts too, I thought. They were little fitted cotton ones with flared legs that gaped very nicely.

We were welcomed into our neighbours' camp, and as Catherine put her arms around Roger's neck to give him a hug her small breasts were visible beneath her top, and his big hands pawed her waist only inches below them.

Roger had on tight fitting shorts with no underwear. His cock was immediately semi-firm. Liz was sitting with her legs tucked to one side. She had on a floral wrap-around dress tied above her breasts, and from behind her legs I could see a pink gash that looked moist.

We got to drinking and laughing about the events of the day. Catherine gradually relaxed from keeping her

171

arms folded and her legs tucked to one side, and I noticed Roger getting his first look at her pussy. She was lying back on a sun lounger with one leg down and the other bent up. He had edged his chair around so he was facing her with a clear view through the leg of her shorts.

I stayed at Roger's shoulder for a while, and Catherine didn't meet his eyes, but she was blushing and quite obviously knew she was displaying herself.

This absolutely thrilled me. It was the reason I brought my wife here – to let other men have a look at her and hopefully get onto her. Ever since I first met Catherine and saw how much she liked attention, I've dreamt about being the guy with her and watching on while she's being played with and fucked.

It was all falling into place, and for the next hour or so Roger was constantly watching my wife. Whenever she moved, his eyes would flash upon her legs, and there were times he sat staring. When he stood up to take a turn at getting more drinks, his cock was completely erect and stretching the waist band of his shorts.

"Must be that native blood," he joked, and Catherine's blush deepened.

Liz went inside with Roger, and I saw they were having a cuddle.

I met my wife's eyes then looked down at her exposed pussy. "Are you nervous?"

"A little. He's been staring at me."

I bent down and kissed her. I smoothed my hand along her thigh and felt into the leg of her shorts. Her warm little slit was wet, and I teased it open with my fingertips. She moaned into my mouth, but she also pushed against my arm.

"Not here," she uttered softly. "You have to take me home if you want to do that."

"And you're gonna let Roger do it later?" I asked as I kissed her some more. I wanted to make her say yes again – to be sure.

"Yes, I will. If you're certain that's what you want?"

Catherine's eyes closed softly as I tasted her lips again. "You know it's what I want," I groaned, and I felt up under her top and wet a nipple with her pussy juice.

Her head rocked back, so I mauled her neck and lifted her top and sucked her nipple into my mouth.

Catherine's legs scissored, and she took hold of my head, kind of pushing me away but not immediately. "Stop that," she scolded. "What if someone's watching?"

Roger and Liz came back after putting on music, and the night eased into some slow dancing. Another couple joined us, and a little later two more couples and a few single men wandered over from nearby camps. Catherine was a good 10 years younger than anyone else, and all of the men were watching her, but she had avoided sitting down since the first couple arrived, and mostly she was hiding behind my shoulder.

I didn't feel much like dancing, but I was happy to start offering my lovely wife up to each of the other men. They were gentlemanly. They would hold her close and feel her back, but I didn't see any of them try to go any further until after we announced we were leaving and Roger claimed her for one last dance. He was holding her close and swaying to the music. He'd gotten in beneath her arms, which were resting loosely around his neck, and her top had lifted, so her breasts were available beneath it.

They were over the far side where it was quite dark, but I could see the guy's big hand was stroking the underside of my wife's tit – just sort of feeling the exposed portion. Then he searched up under her little top and gave her nipple a squeeze and softly rolled it.

I was chatting with one of the other men, but I was watching them over his shoulder. Two other couples were dancing and gazing into each other's eyes. Another woman was chatting with two other men, and they were paying no attention. Liz had been teasing all the men, but one of them had taken her inside the camper, and I thought he may have been fucking her.

Catherine's head was resting beneath Roger's chin, but her eyes were wide. I glanced away when she looked over. Roger's other hand had lowered to the small of her back. He was gently stroking her and caressing beneath the waist band of her shorts. Their slow swaying turned their bodies again, and before Catherine's eyes were upon mine, I saw that Roger had his hand completely under her top.

She met my gaze and I smiled, and she offered an embarrassed little grin in reply.

The song ended, and I saw Roger steal a kiss and a quick little feel of Catherine's crotch before he released her. I didn't know whether the older man had managed to get his fingers into my wife. She seemed to linger just for a moment though, and she was completely flushed when she approached.

I led my wife back to our camper, and as soon as we were in the door we fucked without speaking, ending up lying side by side sweating and spent.

Catherine

I took a breath and looked at my husband. "I've never really been able to say no to men – or even boys when I was in my teens. I just go all weak at the knees and can't seem to stop it from happening, whatever the guy wants!"

Ashton squeezed my hand. "I know, baby. It's a big part of why I love you."

"Oh." I bit down on a grin. "Okay then."

"Yeah, this is perfect for what I want. I love the way you are with pretty much any guy who looks at you, and I don't want you to change."

I was flushing all warm inside now and I melted into my man's kiss.

"It's good, because I don't know if I would have been able to change for long, Ashton. It's not like I can think and decide anything. As soon as a man looks at me that way, I feel compelled to submit to him. And if one of them goes further and touches me, there's nothing I can do about it, I need to do what he says."

"Aw fuck, baby, really? That's so fucking hot."

"Mmm, I know it is, and I'm all yours don't forget. Anytime you want sex, you're the same as other men and I'll do whatever you say."

Ashton stroked my face, studying my eyes. "Okay, so it sounds like I need to be careful not to put you in any situation with other men that I don't want to happen."

I smiled. "Um, yes, exactly! You won't be able to blame me now that I've told you, and it wouldn't be fair to blame the other man... since I'm a total slut and really easy... and as if any man can resist temptation, right?"

"Can't imagine any man resisting you, baby. No fucking way!"

I giggled. "Hmm, but don't worry, I have boundaries. Not in front of children and not in public, unless it's a nude beach and everyone's doing it haha."

My husband frowned his next question. "And what about married men cheating on their wives?"

"Um.." I grimaced guiltily. "I can't help it if a man's being bad, and if he touches me I won't be able to resist."

"I see, that's fair enough. And what about male relatives, has any of them ever..?"

"Um no, and I wouldn't let any of my relatives... only yours!" I said and blushed guiltily. "You might need to look after me at any family parties, especially if your uncle's there!"

"Oh shit, I really am going to have to look after you, aren't I, baby."

"Uh huh," I breathed into another kiss. "But if you want me to start letting the men here get more friendly with me, I can do that."

"Aw jeez, babe, I want that so bad," my husband groaned desperately. "I'd fucking love to see some other man get with you!"

Ashton

The next day at the beach my intriguing new wife again wore a bikini, but it was just a tiny string with a few triangle patches. After a swim Liz went back to get some shopping done, and I lay down with Roger stretched out on the other side of Catherine. She was on her belly and had undone her top. After a while she lifted to her elbows, and I noticed her top slip from beneath her tits.

"You don't want that, do you?" Roger asked, his voice low and playful.

"No, I guess not," Catherine answered, and she looked at me but I pretended to be asleep, and she soon turned away again.

Roger sat up and began applying sunscreen. He only covered his arms and face, then he started rubbing some into Catherine's back. He was on his knees beside her, and he smoothed it over her shoulders. He squirted more of the fluid and rubbed it into his palms, then he smoothed his hands up Catherine's sides with his fingers flaying over her tits.

I felt my wife's eyes upon me again but only for a moment. She laid her head down on her folded arms. The older man had settled to massaging her gently, smoothing his hands down her back then palming her sides with his fingers searching beneath. He'd been feeling the roundness of her breast with each stroke, and after a little bit Catherine lifted for him.

She was looking around, but we were quite secluded between sand dunes. "There's no one watching," Roger assured, and he reached beneath her body and cupped her breasts and felt them properly. He rubbed her nipples then squeezed her fully in his big hands. Catherine lifted to her elbows again. Her eyes closed and she bit down on her lip.

Roger's cock was standing upright. It was virtually throbbing and there was pre-cum oozing from the tip. He kept feeling a tit with one hand, and his other hand smoothed down Catherine's back again, and that time he felt over her bottom and between her legs, but she squirmed onto her side, pushing at his arm.

"It's okay, no one's watching." Roger assured and felt into her crotch again, but she clung to his wrist.

"No, not here. Not like this," she whispered urgently. "Just wait and I'll do something for you, okay?"

My wife's body was being groped openly now, and I was tingling all over with excitement and anticipation.

Roger had his hand firmly wedged between her legs, his fingers squelching in her juices. She fumbled with the sunscreen, squeezing a glob into her palm, and she closed her hand over his cock. He bucked immediately and abandoned her pussy. He held her close, with his wet fingers gripping her hip and his other hand over the back of her head. It looked like he was trying to get her to suck him off, but Catherine's palm was rolling over the head of his cock, and suddenly he convulsed.

Cum lashed Catherine's cheek, but she pressed her fingers over the throbbing head and Roger's load oozed between them. He shuddered and weakened to slump down onto his towel, and Catherine checked around but we hadn't been disturbed.

I could see beneath her body as she leant over and sucked Roger's cock into her mouth. She sucked it softly, cleaning it then licking his cum from her fingers.

"That's right, baby, eat it all," I said, and I met the older man's grin.

Roger was on his back propped on his elbows watching her and looking around to be sure no one came along. A thick glob of semen had seeped from Catherine's fingers and pooled in his ball sac, and she lifted his cock and gathered it with her tongue.

"It's a good wife you've got here, lad."

I nodded. "I'm pleased you're enjoying her. It looks like she loves the taste of your cum."

Catherine moaned softly as she kissed and sucked on the older man's balls, then her tongue trailed back up his shaft and gathered the glob of semen that was oozing from the swollen tip. She smiled up at him, teasing his cock head with her teeth, then she closed her eyes and sucked half his length back into her mouth.

"There's someone coming," I said.

Two women were approaching. Catherine sat up and Roger covered his cock with a towel. "Thanks, love, that was amazing, but I really have to rush if you don't mind. I'm supposed to be meeting Liz to go shopping."

"No, that's okay," Catherine said and was blushing when Rodger left and she lay back down. She met my eyes and questioned me with her smile. I gave her hand a squeeze, and she leaned to me tentatively and met my lips.

Her lips were tacky, her breath thick with the scent of the other man's cum, but I kissed her softly, and she moaned into my mouth, extending her warm, salty tongue as evidence of what she had done to please me.

"Are you satisfied now?" she whispered softly. "Did you like watching me do that?"

"There's still cum on your face, baby. It's all down the side and on your neck."

"I know. I can feel it." Catherine giggled. "Now I really *am* marked." She touched the splotch of goo that crossed her cheek and the corner of her mouth, stringing between her lips when they parted. She leant across to be kissed again, and I met her open mouth and warm, salty tongue, willingly allowing the semen on her lip to become part of our kiss.

Catherine

I felt my face when I moved back to my own towel. "I'm going to just lie here with it like this so you can see what he did, okay?"

Ashton nodded, and I lay on my belly with my head turned towards him and my hair pulled back from my face so he could see.

I also had the quite strong taste in my mouth and the feel of semen coating my teeth. I don't know what it is about older men, but they taste much more potent to me, and I really enjoy that. I guess it's because of their maturity – like smelly old bulls or whatever.

I swallowed again at the powerful taste and the scent of the older man filling my senses. I was on my front but lifted high enough on my elbows that any men walking by would be able to see my breasts.

I only have small boobs, but men seem to like them well enough, and before long there were several old pervert ones sitting around on the sand looking at me.

I rolled eyes and smiled at my husband. "Should I turn over for them?"

Ashton gulped and nodded. "Go on, baby, let them have a look."

I got up on my knees and stretched my towel – the men's eyes riveted to me immediately. I let them enjoy the view of my little peaks pointing down like that for a moment, then I sat and rested back on my hands, facing them fully but with my head turned away.

My nipples were tight and I had to measure breaths because it always excites me so much being looked at sexually.

I kept looking out towards the ocean but after a while I dared to turn my head and look at the men. There were five of them now, and I looked down at my tits and directly around at them all, inviting them to stare all they wanted.

I was entering a weird, funky state of mind that was all too common... one where inhibitions faded and if a man told me to spread my legs, I would.

Of course none of the men asked me to do anything, or even approached and tried to touch me with my husband sitting there beside me, but if only they knew what they could do with me if they wanted.

When I get like this, I'm a complete ragdoll.

I just can't help it.

"Okay let's get going," my husband said after an hour of me being ogled and crowded closer to, and I stood and kind of snapped out of my trance to put an arm across my breasts and blush around at the twelve dirty old men I counted – some of them glaring intently and no doubt fucking me in their mind, rather than just smiling their pleasure.

Ashton

That night Liz had on a tiny skirt that flashed her pussy and a string bikini top that just covered her nipples. Catherine was bare beneath one of my tee-shirts. Roger was completely naked, and I had on only a pair of thin cotton shorts. We were having a few drinks before dinner when two men approached and said hello. They were both naked.

Catherine immediately blushed. The tee-shirt wasn't long enough to cover her pussy when she was sitting, and both men had positioned themselves in front of her. They were talking with Liz and Roger, making plans to visit later that evening.

"Hey, I know that guy," I whispered to Catherine. "Mike Creed. His son and I were kind of friends at school."

"That's freaky. What are the chances of bumping into someone so far from home?"

"I know…. I'm sure it's him. He was a real arsehole. He used to tease the hell out of me when I was a kid."

The two visitors both glanced at Catherine's legs, and while the older one was talking, the younger one, a balding man of about 40, turned his head quite casually and stood staring at her crotch.

I leaned a little to the side so I could see past him. Catherine was sitting with her knees almost touching, but between them there was a clear view of the length of her slit. She rubbed her thighs, tempted to pull her tee-shirt down, it seemed. The guy was just staring at her. He was completely out of the conversation. He seemed to be in a daze, and Catherine was trying not to meet his eyes.

Roger looked over at me and smiled. The guy's cock began to firm. It flexed and lifted away from his body. It expanded and lengthened, and Catherine went bright red as she tried to keep nodding and smiling at Liz and the other guy.

"Ashton? It's you, isn't it?" The man I recognised approached.

"Hey, Mr Creed."

Mike Creed chuckled. "It *is* you, eh? Imagine bumping into young weasel in a place like this. He used to hang around with my son," he explained to the others. "He was always a skinny little runt. Looks like he's grown up."

"Yeah, I grew up," I agreed, chuckling along nervously. The man still intimidated me a little.

"Looks like you married well, though," Mike went on, nodding down at Catherine.

She blushed up at him, smiling shyly. He tilted his head to have a look under her tee-shirt. She was sitting forward, but Roger kneaded her shoulders and she peered up at him. She also leant back, resting on her hands, and with the hem of her tee-shirt lifting slightly.

Roger whispered something, making Catherine giggle. Mike and his friend were both examining her cunt. Mike glanced at me and winked. "Nice," he said, smirking.

Catherine turned back to blush up at the guys again. She looked down at herself, smoothing her tee-shirt over her belly and fiddling with the hem. She didn't cover herself. She just peered back up at the two men.

Roger was distracted, talking with his wife. Mike's friend left to respond to someone calling him from their camp. Mike placed an arm around my shoulder and gripped me. "Yeah, you've done very well for yourself. We don't get a lot of pretty young things like this here," he said, smiling at Catherine again.

Catherine bit down on her grin. The older man tilted his head to have another look at her cunt. She plucked at the hem of her shirt, fiddling with it and meeting my gaze as she folded it up a little, showing herself properly.

"Yeah, that's nice. Shaved is how we like them eh, son?" Mike gave my shoulder a squeeze and shook me encouragingly. He winked at Catherine. "Don't worry, love, me and your hubby here go back a long way. He won't mind me checking you out."

I felt my face was red as I forced a smile.

"Come on, one more little look before I have to go, eh?" the guy went on, winking at Catherine again.

Catherine blushed deeply as she held my eyes and lifted the bottom of her shirt up to her belly. She tucked it under to keep it there and rested back. "Yeah, that's nice," Mike Creed groaned, and as I looked down at what

Catherine was doing, she parted her legs a little for the guy.

Mike's cock flexed. He took hold of it and held it to one side as it quickly expanded. He smiled. "Oops!"

I chuckled nervously, my shoulder being gripped and shaken amusingly. Catherine watched me being jostled. She kept her legs open for the older man, parting them a tiny bit further when he looked back down at her.

"That's a pretty little pussy, love," he said, his voice even now.

Catherine blushed a bit deeper. "Thank you." She looked down at herself and tugged her tee-shirt up above her breasts, opening her thighs a little more as she met my gaze again.

"Fuck yeah!" Mike groaned. "Very fucking nice. Just lie back a bit further, love. Let's have a good look at you eh!"

"Uh huh," Catherine uttered, and she lay all the way back, keeping hold of her tee-shirt. She let her legs part either side of the chair and rested propped on one elbow, just peering up at the man looking at her body.

I gulped, my voice raspy as I spoke. "We haven't been married long yet. We're still almost newly-weds."

"Yeah? You should have invited me to the wedding. I could have helped out afterwards." Mike gripped his cock and shook it. "What do you think, love?"

Catherine's blush deepened again. "Um... I don't know about on our wedding night exactly."

"It's a huge surprise that you're here now though, Mr Creed." I cleared my throat. "I guess I'm mostly glad that you are. It's a bit strange seeing someone we know, but it's an exciting kind of bad."

"Haha, the best kind of bad, son. It's gonna be fun bumping into you back home too after this – knowing what your wife looks like under her clothes." The guy tilted to look closely between Catherine's legs. "Ooh that's nice." He glanced back at me. "Is she a good tight fuck?"

I gulped and nodded. "Yeah, she is," I answered while meeting my wife's blush.

"Yeah that's it, keep your legs spread. Oh yeah it looks tight. Is it, love?"

"Mmm, I hope I'd be tight for you," Catherine answered sweetly, and she bent up one leg onto the chair and swayed it open. "Is that wide enough?"

"Aw fuck yeah," the guy groaned and quickly checked around.

"Maybe it *would* have been fun if you were at our wedding," Catherine teased, directed at me.

"Yeah maybe," I croaked.

"Could have taught you how to fuck her good, son. Could have given you lessons eh!"

"Yeah you could have," I agreed, feeling how red my face must have been.

The man chuckled. "I'll drop by one day then. You can model your wedding dress for me, love."

"Hmm okay," Catherine uttered, smiling as she pressed her legs together.

There was suddenly laughter and an older couple were approaching. Catherine quickly sat up and stretched down her shirt. Roger returned and Mike nodded to him. "So, we'll call back around after dinner," he said.

"Good, Mike. See you then."

Mike strolled away, winking at me and slapping my back.

Ashton

After dinner things settled with some music and more drinks. Catherine and I cuddled, swaying together through a few songs.

"So, what about that guy Mike?" Catherine asked.

"I know. He's always been like that. He doesn't like me and the feeling's mutual."

"I noticed. But I didn't mind him looking at me." Catherine lifted to whisper, "Did you like me spreading my legs like that?"

"Yeah, except I wasn't sure about it with him exactly. I bet he enjoyed it with you being my wife."

"I know, but I hope he comes back. He feels so strong and confident – just the look in his eyes. I'd love to do that again for him in front of you."

"Yeah, I don't want it to change anything, sweetheart. I still want you to be sexy."

"You do?"

"Yeah, it might be hard for me to watch him with you at all, but I don't want that to bother you."

Roger approached and cut in with a big smile. I went and sat with Liz, watching them dance. Roger worked his hand from Catherine's hip to her thigh, and with her resting against his shoulder he felt her crotch. Their dancing was just swaying gently together, and Roger was toying with her pussy while her soft little fingers closed over the head of his cock.

I looked at Liz. She had her hand between her legs. I didn't know whether she was inviting me or not, and I felt almost rude by not responding. Catherine and I hadn't spoken about full swinging though, and regardless of what happened between her and other men, I couldn't imagine being with another woman in front of her. I knew she would be upset by that.

I thought Liz understood as we exchanged glances and smiles. She closed her eyes, and I turned back to watch my wife pinned against the camper with her legs apart and old Roger on his knees eating her out. Catherine was looking around anxiously. She was obviously nervous about people from the other camps watching.

Roger took her hand and led her inside, and when I walked in, I saw Catherine on the bed with her legs spread and Roger on top of her. He was thrusting slowly and methodically, and I could see the older man's cock stretching my wife open. She was moaning against his shoulder, and he was gasping with each surge of his body, until she suddenly convulsed. Then he held her and waited for her to settle. He started fucking her again, with his deep thrusts gradually quickening, and just as Catherine's body convulsed again, his old balls clenched and started to throb.

I watched the guy's big hairy testicles intensely. I could see them gently pulsing with each spurt of semen they were injecting into my new wife's belly. Her legs rested wide open as she accepted the deposit. She was peering from the older man's shoulder. I met her eyes and questioned her with a look, glancing again at where she was coupled with the guy. She gave a tiny nod, biting her lip and opening her legs a bit wider.

Roger must have felt that because he resumed screwing her slowly. His bottom was rolling back then clenching as it rolled forward. I sat down on the bed next to them, and Catherine reached for my hand.

Roger arched back and took his cock in his fist. He pressed the head against Catherine's pussy and rubbed it into her. He opened her with it, slicing between her swollen lips and exposing her pink inner folds dripping with semen. He worked the head in and out and rubbed it over her clit. "I hope it was all right to cum in her," he said, meeting my eyes with a grin. "You don't mind other men servicing your wife, do you, lad?"

I shook my head. "You're actually the first since we got married. It's something I need to get used to yet, but not using a condom is okay."

Roger winked at Catherine. "Good, I prefer bareback."

Catherine smiled. "Me too. It was so nice when you came just now."

Roger soon regained his erection, and Catherine squeezed my hand, her eyes closing as the other man's sunk his length back into her. He opened her legs wide again, but Liz came in with the two men from earlier, and as Roger turned to see who it was, his cock slipped out and levered at his waist.

Catherine whimpered softly as the men approached and looked over Roger's shoulder. She had pulled her tee-shirt down, but Roger kept her legs spread wide, and the younger of the two men quickly developed a hard-on while Mike started massaging his cockhead.

Roger was edging back. "Can these guys have some as well?" he asked both me and Catherine.

"Can we have a few minutes alone first?" I replied.

Roger left us, pulling an expandable partition across to give us privacy.

I looked to my wife. "Do you wanna, sweetheart?"

"I don't know," she whispered back. "You don't even like that older one."

"I know. He's gonna take great pleasure in screwing you in front of me too. And now that I think about it, I actually did mention to his son Bradley that I was gonna bring you here this week. He probably came here to get a look at you."

"So, that's even more reason not to go this far with him, isn't it?"

I stroked my wife's face and kissed her softly. "I think I still want it to happen, sweetheart. It'll be embarrassing for me, but I still want it."

Catherine blushed. "Hmm, that's kind of hot. Being taken by my husband's enemy."

"Well, let's do it, then?" I went on anxiously. "Before I chicken out and change my mind."

"Okay, but no messy creampies? I'd rather they cum all the way inside, as deep in my belly as they can."

I nodded. I got up and pulled back the partition. The men were all waiting at the other end of the mobile home. They approached. I stepped aside. "Okay, but just one at a time," I said to them, meeting Mike's eyes and smirk.

The younger guy immediately got into position between Catherine's legs. "So, don't need a rubber?"

"No," I replied. "As long as you keep your dick in her nice and deep when you're unloading."

"Especially if there's going to be three of you," Catherine added, peering around at everyone. "Try and cum inside me as deep as you can, please."

The guy's cock was short and thick, the head huge. He only crouched down. He didn't lie over her – probably because I was sitting there at her shoulder. Catherine clung to my hand and to the bottom of her tee-shirt, keeping it pulled down to her belly.

The guy groaned as he sunk his cock into her. He was balls deep, and he started slowly rolling his hips, surging as far up her as he could reach. "Fuck she's hot!" he cried as he withdrew, and his cock popped out and sprung upright. Then he crouched again and tried to spear it back into her, but it slipped up over her clit. He pulled back again and poked at her a few times, and when he got the head in he immediately ground himself hard against her.

"Man, she's so fucking wet," he gasped, and started pounding her. He was jolting her body and grimacing with each thrust. He had his hands beneath Catherine's knees, and he lifted her and spread her legs wider. "Fuck – here it is!" he yelled, and he jammed himself hard against her again, and Catherine crushed my hand as the other man's head shot back.

"Fuck yeah!" The man gripped Catherine's thighs and pulled her firmly against his body, holding her there and pumping his load into her. Catherine's fingers loosened their grip within mine, and I softly stroked her hand with my thumb. That guy pulled out of her and backed away, and Mike moved into position between her legs.

I smoothed my wife's forehead and kissed her lips. "Are you sure this is okay?"

"Uh huh," she uttered. "I like it with one man after another having me."

She was clinging to me and trying to bury her head into my neck. Her body started rocking back and forth though, and I stayed there with her, kissing and stroking her face. But she was soon being jolted again, and I lifted from her and moved back a little.

Mike lay down on top of her and her legs fell away as he started humping. He grinned up at me. "That's better. Just sit back and watch me fuck your pretty wife."

"Okay," I said, meeting Catherine's blush. "Cum in her really deep too, okay?"

"I intend to," the guy replied, meeting my eyes again and holding them as he pressed his lips to Catherine's. She met his kiss, and I saw the guy insert his tongue into her mouth. He was on his elbows holding her head in place while he continued tongue-kissing her. He was thrusting slowly with his hips, rolling them and fucking her deeply.

I met my wife's eyes and held her gaze as she opened her mouth wide for the man on top of her. He had lifted from kissing her, and he traced his tongue around her lips. Her mouth was wet from his saliva. He covered it again and mashed hard, making Catherine moan.

The guy lifted his upper body and looked at me. "She's got a sexy mouth too. Bet she gives good head."

I nodded. "I'm sure she wouldn't mind demonstrating for you later."

The guy chuckled and felt Catherine's tits. "These feel good too, eh?"

"Pull her shirt up," Roger said. He was working his full erection.

Mike stretched Catherine's tee-shirt above her tits, and he held himself up and watched them bounce while he fucked her with short, powerful jolts. He was getting close, though. His eyes were bulging and they were suddenly glazed. He started grunting, and his thrusts were slow and deep. His body tensed and he let out a loud groan and buried his cock into her as far as he could.

I held my wife's blank, submissive gaze as her body was being injected with more semen. Her hand was still lightly touching mine, and her other hand was above her head with her fingers twirling absently in her hair.

Mike seemed to be ejaculating for a long time, and when he finally finished he spent a moment enjoying the feel of her. He was slowly rolling his hips, and he started groping her tits and sucking on them.

His friend was playing with Liz. He had her against the wall with his hand under the front of her skirt. They left together.

Mike lifted from Catherine but remained coupled with her. "Your wife's a good fuck, Ashton." He ground into her and pumped a few times. "Damn she's tight." He smiled at Catherine's blush. "You feel good, baby."

"Uh huh… You can cum in me again if you want."

He grinned. "Yeah. I want." He resumed fucking her, thrusting hard and making her tits bounce again. He lifted one leg and held it to his chest, twisting her sideways and pounding against her. Roger and I were watching his dick spear in and out. "Fuck yeah," he cried, and he jammed himself hard against her and held firm once more. "Take it, baby. Take that load," he taunted. "Yeah, that's it – that's a fucking belly full right there, man." He looked at me. "That's your wife's little sexy belly all full of cum."

I stroked Catherine's face. The guy's dick oozed out of her. He pulled up his pants. "So, tomorrow then, eh? I wanna fuck her again, okay, man?"

I nodded, my face red. "Okay."

Mike winked at Catherine then rushed off. "Catch ya later, Roger."

Catherine closed her legs but only loosely. She was peering up at Roger. He knelt on the bed and guided her onto her side as he got behind her. He rubbed the swollen head of his cock into her gooey little gash, and she whimpered softly as he penetrated her. "Do you want me to suck you while he has me again?" she asked me.

Roger guided her to her knees and I knelt in front. Her mouth closed over my cock as Roger bumped against her, holding her hips and thrusting. I remained still and let the older man rock my wife's body back and forth. Then Roger reached beneath and groped her tits. He started humping her deep and hard, and I could feel his thrusts jolting through her. When Roger shot his load into Catherine's belly, I flooded her mouth.

Catherine swallowed then released my cock and laid her head against my hip. I stroked her hair while Roger massaged the back of her neck and slowly ground against her bottom.

"Come over for breakfast?" Roger asked.

"I guess," I answered.

Roger withdrew and felt into Catherine. She moaned softly and ground back against him. He cupped her crotch and started rubbing her. I didn't know if he had fingers in her or if he was just working her clit, but she soon convulsed in orgasm.

"Not too early. Maybe around 10?" Roger said. He lifted Catherine, his big hands up her tee-shirt. "Are you going to indulge tomorrow?" he asked, kissing her neck.

She shook her head. "Never!"

Roger laughed, and he left to go and *rescue* Liz.

Catherine

Ashton lay next to me, and I tugged my tee-shirt down and cuddled up to his chest. He was stroking my hair and we just lay quietly for a long moment. Eventually I lifted and whispered into his ear, "I felt all three of them actually spurting in me and my belly is so full of their cum."

"Is it?" My husband placed his hand upon my belly. "It's freaky but exciting to think that three other men have deposited, well, their genetic material I guess it amounts to." He stroked my hair with his other hand. "Three other men have now been between my wife's legs and taken their pleasure."

"Uh huh – they *did* take their pleasure," I whispered. "It's going to be exciting seeing them around tomorrow, when they look at me and remember being inside me."

"Like Uncle does?" Ashton asked, meeting my lips softly.

"Yes, like that, just like your uncle remembers every time we see him."

"Yeah, well, maybe we should let him refresh his memory sometime. Would you like that, sweetheart?"

"Okay," I moaned into another kiss. "If you want to invite him over one night, I'll let him have me again. You could pretend to be called away and leave me at home alone with him. He could make another one of those huge deposits inside my belly, just like these men did." I held my husband's hand to my belly and whispered teasingly, "Since my husband doesn't mind other men servicing me."

"Yeah, true," he said, his face reddening a little. "We'll just need to be careful that one of them doesn't actually service you thoroughly, if you know what I mean."

"Hmm, that's true," I agreed. "We wouldn't want some other man's genetic material getting with mine while I'm fertile," I added with a giggle. "That wouldn't be good."

"So, there's no danger of that right now is there, sweetheart?"

"No. Doc wants me to go off the pill again for a while, but I'm still on it at the moment."

"Oh, okay. That's good. We should let Uncle before you go off it then. We could invite him over one night next week?"

"All right. Next week would be perfect. That's the end of my month, so after that I can go off the pill and we'll just have to be really careful with timing with any other men, unless they use condoms."

"Okay, of course. So we'd still be able to let another guy cum in you, but not when you're um…"

"Not when I'm ovulating," I finished for my man, blushing at the thought. "There will still be some safe times each month if you want to let another guy be with me unprotected."

Ashton took my hand, intertwining fingers. He rolled onto his side facing me. "I think I'd prefer it unprotected so they get to cum inside you like these guys did. As long as we're careful about who we decide on, maybe find a couple of regular boyfriends for you... I dunno if it'd be a good idea to let Uncle fuck you too often, maybe once every now and then."

"He obviously hasn't told anyone. At least he's discreet," I said. "Discreet is good."

"True! Older single men are probably the best candidates. They'll be so thrilled to get a chance with you, they won't wanna ruin it by blabbing or bragging."

I blushed. "Uh huh, and older men are experienced too... I like that."

Ashton chuckled. "Good point, sweetheart. Hopefully I'll get to watch and learn sometimes."

"Yes, I will always enjoy it more if you're watching," I said into a kiss, and I lay there cuddling and kissing my new husband, thrilled to have my pussy full and leaking sperm from three other men. I was absolutely glowing inside from that, and with Ashton being such a willing cuckold, I knew I would be getting fucked by these other men again tomorrow. I hoped I would also get the chance to suck their cocks.

I just love sucking cocks and the feel of cum being spurted in my mouth.

I turned over for my husband to cuddle closer to me, and I snuggled back against him content in the knowledge that although married now, I was free to continue being the slut that I am.

** The End **

Made in the USA
Monee, IL
24 May 2025

18093022R00125